The Dandy

Peter Gethers

BANTAM BOOKS · TORONTO · NEW YORK · LONDON

THE DANDY
A Bantam Book / published by arrangement with
E P DUTTON

PRINTING HISTORY
E. P. Dutton edition published May 1978
Bantam edition / June 1980

Bantam Books are published by Bantam Books, Inc. Its trademark, consisting of the words "Bantam Books" and the portrayal of a bantam, is Registered in U.S. Patent and Trademark
Office and in other countries. Marca Registrada. Bantam
Books, Inc., 666 Fifth Avenue, New York, New York 10019

To my parents, who fed, edited, and supported.

We are today legatees of the Victorian ambivalence. In our dissatisfaction with utopia we marvel at the *possibility* of ignoring progress, despising community and adoring self. We are tired of rubbing shoulders with humanity. But the dandy, who made a success (however despicable and trivial) of absolute selfishness, is now merely a nostalgic catchword in the poet's lexicon.

From *The Dandy: Brummell to Beerbohm*

Part One

1.

"It's a funny thing."

"What?"

Eugene Toddman looked down at the girl, at her arms, which were not too chubby and were soft, pale with a handful of freckles. The arms were new to him, he had met her that day at a wedding; now she was without her shirt. The girl was an instructor at the Fred Astaire School of Dance and she came close to having a dancer's body. She also had an unpleasant nasal voice and a lip that did something funny. It curled up to reveal part of her gum, so she seemed always about to whine. She had a very nice long neck, though, which now twisted down. She rubbed her chin across the top of her chest; her breasts shook, barely moving, from side to side. She looked at him.

"What's a funny thing?" the girl asked.

Eugene glanced at his own body. He smiled at the girl. His

eyes narrowed and he shrugged. Eugene Toddman thought about the first time he had ever been to France.

At sixteen he had hitched all over Europe. When he passed through the Loire Valley it was the end of the summer, hot but pleasant; the kind of weather that makes you squint at the sun, and sniff and smile, and put on sunglasses to look out over the swaying countryside. Eugene had been on the road for three months and was feeling loose and relaxed and confident. He needed nothing; content, with each new ride, just to lean his head back and listen to the French farmers, doctors, truckdrivers ramble on about life. Aware that he had only two days left to get back to Paris if he were to catch his plane home, Eugene hopped out of a Citroën to find himself on the outskirts of a small town in the Saumur region. It was twilight; he stood for a moment on the side of the road before taking the few steps to a faded *degustation* sign. A beaten down path led to a warped door built into the side of a hill. Eugene followed the trail till its end and went down into a family winery. He stood at the bar, had a glass of cold *rosé*. The *cave* was chilly and damp; Eugene ran his finger over the moss on the stone walls. The bartender left him, went to drink *Pernod* and lemon syrup with cronies at one of the scattered round tables. Eugene reached over the bar, took an unopened bottle, tucked it under his arm. He dropped three francs fifty into a saucer, returned a nod from the owner, and went back outside. It was dark and had gotten windy. Looking around, Eugene saw a couple of small boys on bicycles and a woman carrying a long loaf of bread. Pastry trays were half-filled with extraordinary works of art. Laundry hung above winding cobblestone streets. Elaborate grille-work balconies decorated bombed-out houses. Street noises—voices and footsteps and muffled mechanical sounds—filtered in to him. He walked a little way to a small hotel, half-expecting Truffaut to pop out from an alleyway with a hand-held camera. Real life faded into a cinematic vision . . . a rippling, sepia-tinted longshot.

CLOSEUP: Three wooden steps. Grainy. Knotty. Uneven.

EXTERIOR: The rickety front porch to the hotel.

A peel of white paint here and there. A rocking chair.

INTERIOR: The hotel.

A lobby filled with comfortable furniture, a few cats and an old woman with crooked fingers behind the desk.

"Bonsoir, monsieur."

"Bonsoir, madame. Vous avez une chambre?"

"Pour deux?"

Eugene shook his head regretfully and held up one finger. When the woman nodded, Eugene gave her his bottle of wine and asked her to keep it cold. He followed her up a narrow spiral stairway to a little storybook room with a slanted ceiling, a high brass bed covered by a patchwork quilt and down pillows. A chest, overflowing with ancient, leatherbound books, stood next to the bed; colorfully mismatched china plates rested upright in a hutch. Once alone, Eugene sat gingerly on top of the quilt, then eased himself back to rest against the pillows. He watched darkness move, absolutely, across the room, and he dozed off with his clothes on. Around ten, he woke up, rolled his eyes, and chewed his lips in the way of a disoriented traveler; put some water on his face and tried to swallow away the crust on his tongue and the dryness on the roof of his mouth. Then strolled down to the lobby. The old woman was now sitting in front of the desk, watching a black-and-white television. She handed Eugene a chocolate and asked if he'd had dinner.

"Non," he admitted. *"C'est possible?"*

She clucked as she shuffled into the kitchen. When she returned, she said that leftovers were being warmed. Waiting, they talked for a little while, intimately swapping tales of his travels and the people who came to her hotel. Soon, the old woman pinched at a loosely hung stocking and went back into the kitchen to get the food. A tray was brought out instead by a young girl with straight, light-brown hair. The girl placed in front of Eugene a platter of rabbit stewed in mustard sauce. There was also spinach and zucchini, dark, strong coffee, and bread. The girl sat down with him, poured his wine, now cold, and asked Eugene to light her cigarette, which he did expertly.

She worked at the hotel, this girl. She was half-Dutch and half-Norwegian, taking odd jobs wherever she felt like staying while she saw the world. She was nineteen years old, spoke a lovely, broken, academic English which she needlessly kept apologizing for, wore a short dress that barely covered shiny tanned legs; she was beautiful. They talked for several hours, quietly and easily, she revealing a curious nature and a mischievous smile, he sipping several brandies and smoking small cigars she had brought. Sometime after one, Eugene asked for an alarm clock, saying that he had to get up at five so he could catch the truckdrivers heading toward Paris. The girl said that there were no alarm clocks.

"I am up early, always," she said. "I will wake you. I have something in my teeth."

He watched her nail slip into her mouth, flick against a tooth, and then she was smiling at him. She put one foot up on the table and they talked a bit more. Eugene sipped yet another brandy, smiled back, almost to himself, blew a smoke ring, leaned back leisurely. The beautiful girl told him how cold it would be at five in the morning.

"Brrr," she said. And shivered.

Eugene shrugged, scratched his left cheek, covered a yawn, and knew she was looking into his bloodshot eyes, the lids half closed.

"Brrr," she said again, and said what a shame it was that her room was so far from his. "The hallway is cold, walking at five in the morning."

Eugene nodded, cleared his throat, squeezed his teeth over the rim of the brandy glass, and slowly opened his eyes. The girl said she was going to her room, would he like to come? Eugene said uh huh, he would, more than anything he could think of, and walked back with this wonderful girl to her tiny secluded quarters, where he ran his hands over her perfect shoulders, slid his fingers up and down her arms, and lifted off her dress, all the while grinning the grin of a madman who had stumbled mistakenly into sanity. Her head curled onto his body, his arm under her as they fell asleep, their legs intertwined beneath the single sheet, and she, as promised, woke him at five. While he rubbed his eyes, trying to understand why he had been allowed a glimpse of heaven, the girl brought up a steaming pot of coffee, an earthenware pitcher of hot, thick milk, and a croissant made with homemade peach butter. Eugene sleepily ran his thumb along her cheek and kissed her lightly, his tongue lingering just an instant inside her upper lip. He got out of bed, dressed, smiled a soft farewell, his eyes shining, and stepped out into the quiet, cool dawn; walked away down the still-dark country road toward Paris.

Fourteen years later Eugene was in New York, with this dance instructor he had met at this wedding. After the ceremony, she said she had to pick something up at work, so he went with her and stood around in the marble-columned waiting room. He watched an old man who wore one of the world's worst toupees glide through a waltz with a woman whose feet were covered with Band-Aids. A fat girl, a teen-ager, smiled at Eugene, and this other woman, around forty and dressed all in black, was busy running her hand up and down her thigh and calf. There was a blind man attempting to learn the foxtrot. There were a few fags in dinner jackets who kept moving from couple to couple saying "slow . . . slow . . . quickquick." One screamer asked Eugene if he was being helped. Eugene nodded.

"Da daaaaa," said the girl as she popped in front of him, her leg dramatically draped around one of the columns. "I'm ready."

Eugene lowered his eyes and smiled and they went for a drink, which stretched into three, in a hotel lobby. Very plush.

"I'm from the Bronx," she said.

"Yeah," said Eugene.

"I wonder why they call it *the* Bronx," she said. "I mean, they don't call it *the* Manhattan, or *the* Queens."

Eugene ordered another drink, and when he finished they went for dinner. Chinese.

"It was a nice wedding, donja think?" she asked.

There was a piece of fried rice on her chin and Eugene was hoping it would fall down onto her tits.

"Oh sure."

Her tongue caught the rice but substituted a squared-off piece of pork.

"She's a great kid."

"Great." Eugene nodded. "Great."

After the almond cookies she put up a bit of an argument when he suggested going down to his place.

"I should go home, really. It's a long trip."

"Don't bother. You can stay at my place."

"Oh no. I should get back."

"Okay."

"Would it put you out?"

"No."

"I should get back."

"Okay."

"Well . . . do you have an extra room?"

At his apartment, he showed her the extra room and she went straight into his bedroom and unbuttoned her shirt.

"He wants a baby," she said.

"Who?"

"Casey. The groom."

"Oh. Yeah. I know."

She was taking off a stocking. She coiled the nylon around her ankle and then let it drop off her toes.

"You think she wants a baby?"

"Sure."

"You think so?"

She was on her back, her legs up, perfectly together, at a forty-five-degree angle, and she pulled off her pants. He could see that she had a nice ass.

"Sure," he said. "Everybody wants a baby, don't they?"

"Do you want a baby?"

"No."

Eugene's shirt was off now, and his shoes and socks. He stepped out of his pants and stood over her. Her heel touched his leg.

"Do you respect women?" she asked.

Kneeling on the bed, he stopped.

"What?"

"Do you respect women?"

"No," he said. "I don't respect anybody."

The girl held out her arms.

"Love me to death," she said to Eugene Toddman.

2.

Eugene had been born with death hanging over him, in a manner of speaking. He had been a premature birth; two months early, he was anxious to burst forth into the world. Then, at the last moment, it was as if he changed his mind and decided that he'd pass on the bursting, that he really was in no hurry, after all, to take the plunge. His indecision proved fatal to his mother. According to the doctor, Eugene was born three seconds before Lavinia Toddman died. No one said anything as the cord was cut and Eugene's first act of life was to cry.

To his credit, Eugene's father didn't hold it against Eugene that Lavinia, his bride of nine years, was not around to be a mother to his child. Morton Toddman sobbed deeply at the funeral, drank heavily for eight days, let his beard grow, then, with a somewhat melancholy and fatalistic hangover, decided that life must go on. So he spent his last few dollars on a new wardrobe, an orange Cadillac, and a nurse for his new son. The nurse stayed home with Eugene while Mort, his Cadillac, and his wardrobe started going out with a variety of women.

Mort slept with no one for three months. He was not yet ready for pleasure; he felt dutybound to live miserably in the present, reveling in the joys of the past. Then he met a secretary and rented a hotel room for the night. Mort liked the secretary, he kissed her affectionately in the morning and took her number, but he never called her again. He expediently removed her from his memory, dismissing her first as a dangerous temptation, then as a desired apparition, ultimately as a distant dream. He spent two more months without sex and then picked up a waitress. And then a cashier. Even an actress. And then an old friend who was married to another old friend. Lying next to Mort, the woman asked if he'd enjoyed the sex.

"No," Mort said, and pulled at his lip.

"Why'd you make love to me, then?" the woman breathed.

"I didn't know what else to do."

Father and son lived in an apartment that, devoid of familial femininity, turned somewhat gloomy. It stayed clean and it stayed comfortable, the furniture was the same, the paintings hung steadfast on the walls. But it was stale. And usually empty. Mort never brought his women home, even for a visit or dinner or a chat. Even for a minute. Mort was a young man but he felt old. He had responsibilities—electric bills and a broken hi-fi. He worried about politics. He had memories and stayed awake at night sweating when they grew vague, or nauseous when he just forgot things. He had guilt because if he hadn't fucked his wife she wouldn't have died.

He liked his son, though. Touched him a lot. Held him. Talked to him. Eugene innocently gurgled away in his bassinet while Mort discussed business with him.

"Things look good today, Gene," he'd say. "Things are gonna go." Eugene would belch and Mort would continue. "You'll be rollin' in pablum, kiddo," Mort would say while

his son made funny noises and drooled. Then Mort would
motion to the living room, to the concrete playground outside their window, to the world, and say, "Someday, kid,
this'll all be yours."

Eventually, things went well for Morton in his new life. A
writer, he wrote—and managed to sell. He got a job writing
a soap opera on the day Eugene said his first word, "More."
He won an award for Best Television Play of the Year for a
"Studio One" a day before Eugene took his first step. Money came in, work rolled his way. Women flocked after him.
Suddenly his life had some sort of shape—he didn't have to
decide what to do anymore because everything, seemingly,
was being done for him, presented to him. Things went so
well for Morton Toddman that within five years he was able
to move out of the city and into the suburbs. To celebrate the
move and Eugene's fifth birthday, Morton held a big out-
door barbecue in their new backyard. All of Eugene's little
friends from Manhattan came out dressed as cowboys and
cowgirls. Station wagons were brimming over with mini-
rustlers and wranglers making shooting noises with their
mouths while cocking their stubby little fingers. Eugene
was having a glorious time, particularly when, on this birthday in late spring, it miraculously started to snow. The grass
got wet and slippery. White flakes blurred the vision. All the
cowpokes ran for cover. All the parents grabbed their drinks.
Eugene's father picked up the barbecue and tried to get it
onto the porch. Halfway there, he tripped, and one tiny, hot
coal hopped out of the bin, landing on Mort's arm. Eugene
heard his first swear word—it was "shitfuck"—as the coal
then rolled down Morton Toddman's arm, off his fingertips,
and settled in the back of Tommy Sleuthfield's mother's
skirt. So it was that Eugene, though he was really too young
to appreciate it, also caught his first glimpse of snatch,
when Mrs. Sleuthfield, in a moment of fired-up inspiration,
ripped off her dress and panties that said "Reptile World,
Kansas" on them. Eugene was so excited with the snow and
the funny behavior of the grown-ups that he threw out his
arms in glee, managing to slam his wrist through the porch-
door glass. Blood gushed everywhere. At five years old he
stood there, clutching his right wrist with his left hand, as

though he could prevent any real pain if only he tried hard enough. The big day ended with Eugene, still squeezing, being driven off to the doctor's to get sewn up.

The images that eventually fade together to become childhood were easy and pleasurable for Eugene Toddman. A bird that crashed through a window and was nursed back to health. A fat negro maid with warts who let Eugene play with her snapbeads and hit him on the head with her shoe when he got out of line. A friend's mother who would sing low and off-key and sweetly. A pedal-car with a smashed-in hood where an eight-year-old bully stomped his foot through. The thrill of tossing his first quarter at a toll-booth basket and the triumph of glazing his first ceramic ashtray. Mostly people floating by, though. Aunts who hugged him and fed him and who taught him to play gin rummy. Mort's friends who smelled, always, of tobacco and leather. Teachers' aftershave lotions and friends' cowlicks. Glimpses of a cousin's nipples every time she wore a certain shift. There were few traumas. Few setbacks. Just a pleasant progression.

School started and Eugene's scar on his wrist provided both a distinguishing mark and instant celebrity status. He was naturally popular, had an immediately winning conversational manner that was sharp and smart but not cute. Though not particularly outgoing, he was affectionate. He got along with people. He listened to them. At this young age he tried so hard to understand what was going on around him, tried to match surrounding dialogue with the sensual stimuli that jumped at him like flash cards and so bowled him over. He also happened to be a good kickball player, especially in the clutch, and was mostly fearless at dodgeball. His maid prepared the best sack lunches, he was never forced to wear galoshes, he had absolutely no distrust of the only Puerto Rican in his school, and he was class president twice in a row. A good fielding second baseman, the third-fastest kid in his grade, the first to learn the multiplication table all the way through nine. He couldn't miss.

The first few years, schoolwork was interesting and came easily. Reading came with an instinctual ease, science was a thing of stimulating wonderment. Dick and Jane were intriguing strangers, litmus paper chameleonic magic. By the time the teacher would say, "How much sooner will Car A arrive than Car B if the trip is one thousand miles," Eugene's hand would be waving madly in the air, way before any of the other pencils were finished scribbling over their wide-lined paper. The change from printing to writing in script was terrific, too, and Eugene spent hours getting his capital letters to slant the exact proper amount to the right. He skipped a grade. He learned Morse Code and had special library privileges and his book reports were almost always up on the bulletin board with a red star. Eugene was a Safety Patrol man and wore his criss-crossing harness as if it were the very essence of justice. He was a chalk monitor and got to clap the erasers together, *outside,* twice a day.

"Gene," said Mort one afternoon, "are you happy?"

"Whaddya mean?"

"I mean are you happy?"

"Sure. Why shouldn't I be?"

"Well, a lot of people aren't."

"Why?"

Mort laughed. "There're reasons."

"Like what?"

"People are poor, or hungry, or . . . ohhh . . . or alone, tired. Old. Young. A lot of people are in pain."

"Oh." Eugene thought it was interesting hearing about all these unhappy people. He wondered what they had to do with him.

"Do you like your friends?"

"Sure."

"You're smarter than they are."

Eugene shrugged.

"You've liked your teachers so far."

"Yeah, they're great."

"You'll find out that they're dull. Or faggots. Or short, or something."

"I gotta do my homework, dad."

"Remember that you're happy now, Gene. One day it might matter."

"Okay."

"Never take the past away from other people."

Eugene watched his Irish setter step gingerly up the yellow carpeted stairs. "No. I won't," he said. "Why should I?"

By the fourth grade, teachers were having to invent work for Eugene to keep him constantly occupied—he had a tendency to drift away and follow his childish impulses when left with nothing to do. He'd scribble on history books, read comics, whisper, and send notes. He'd lose himself in the musty smells of his scratched-up desk; his eyes would catch a drop of water and he'd follow, enraptured, as it slid down a pane of glass. He'd sometimes even absent-mindedly start to stroll outside, until the teacher would reprimand him. By the sixth grade, Eugene would finish his work in school as quickly as possible and, to avoid disrupting anything, would sit quietly, caring only to drift away into his own ten-year-old mind. At ten, Eugene's heroes were Thomas Edison, Harriet Beecher Stowe, Alfred E. Neuman, and Willie Mays. Especially Willie. Eugene could sit for hours dreaming about someday reaching the point of beauty that the Say-Hey Kid created climbing the ivy to pull in a sure-fire extra base hit. He thought about Willie digging his spikes into the ground and swinging for the fences. And Willie's cap flying off. And the basket catch. Eugene sometimes thought about TV and superheroes and ray guns. He thought about Joanie, the girl who sat three desks in front of him, one row to the right. He also thought about jerking off, a new and exciting discovery.

All this time, Morton Toddman was becoming more and more successful. He was getting *too* successful, in fact, for

New York suburbia. His neighbors looked upon him with suspicion because he worked at home. He looked down on his neighbors because they voted Republican and didn't spend enough money on their haircuts. The women he was going out with were neither intelligent enough nor sophisticated enough nor *plentiful* enough for his taste. Mort developed a hatred for station wagons, a loathing for power mowers. He hid from the mailman, who always said, "Hiya, Mr. T," and from the kids who wanted to rake the leaves or shovel the snow off the path from the house to the garage. He stayed in the city as often as possible because the Boy Scouts terrified him, the Little League repulsed him, and PTA meetings were on the verge of making him suicidal. Everyone knew what he was doing. He knew what everyone else was doing. People he didn't know—he knew what they were doing. Eugene was already a better bowler than his father was, golf bored Mort to tears. Try as he might, Mort couldn't get a hula hoop to go round his waist more than three times. Even a Dairy Queen chocolate blizzard no longer was a thrilling experience. Morton Toddman now had his suits tailor-made but he didn't know anyone with enough taste to admire the fits. So a once-in-a-lifetime offer to write and produce a big TV show was all the impetus he needed to agree to pack his and Eugene's bags and move to Los Angeles. A fresh start, sweeping aside unpleasant memories as well as casting off a stultifying present. A major breakthrough. A godsend.

And the news of the uprooting came at a good time for the younger Toddman also. Eugene's young friendships were already beginning to wear thin. His teachers were not nearly as thrilled with ten-year-old Eugene as they were with the six-year-old one. And scribbling and comics and whispering no longer stirred him. Joanie still stirred him a little. So when he found out he was to move, Eugene decided that he and Joan should celebrate.

They went out on a wintery afternoon to an ice-skating pond a mile or so from Eugene's house. No one else was skating; it was dusk. Eugene helped lace up Joanie's skates and he felt a fluttering in his stomach which verged on being an erection. The two children skated out into the middle of the pond. It was cold and there was a slight wind that played with their exposed cheeks. A dog bounded around in the snow off to the side. A plane flew overhead, the noise reverberating, hanging in the air. As Eugene slid around the ice in his long underwear and heavy clothes, as he watched the little girl giggle and push her hair out of her eyes, as he imagined sipping a hot chocolate and walking with his arm around her, their sides bumping casually together, Eugene was suddenly exhilarated. He smiled, couldn't help himself. A dopey grin spread over his whole face. He looked up to feel the childish awe of a moment of perfection and he skated over to tell Joanie, to share his glee. Before he reached her, though, ten-and-a-half-year-old Joanie Wainright screamed and fell through a patch of thin ice. Eugene, not more than two feet away from her, watched in helpless bewilderment as his playmate gurgled and thrashed around, turned all blue. He tried to cry out but couldn't. He couldn't move. His jaw vibrated up and down, no sound coming out. His eyes burned as they stayed riveted on the water. His legs were rubbery. A tiny bit of spit dribbled down his chin. Joanie sank and drowned as Eugene stared and watched her die. He didn't move for an hour, watched the occasional bubble rise to the surface, caught glimpses of Joanie's body under the ice. He could see her eyes and he looked closely at her, curiously, noticing the odd angle of her head and the strange shape of her mouth. Joanie's mitten floated at the spot where she disappeared. It got colder and Eugene's teeth started to chatter, spasms shivered through his body. He didn't move, though. Just watched and tried to understand what it was that had happened, what it was he was feeling. No longer terror. No longer pain. They had drained from him. The incredible stifling tension faded. He made his first sound in a long time—a soft harsh gasping for air. He closed his mouth. Totally alone, darkness folding over him, Eugene felt . . . *nothing,* now. His muscles relaxed, his breath eased back, his head tilted down, chin on his chest. His body began to sway, gently rocking back and forth. Eugene looked around and saw calm shadows.

Finally, the mother of a friend wandered by and spotted the boy. She walked over to him, started to speak, and then saw Joanie's mitten. Then she saw Joanie.

Eugene had a couple of months left in New York before the move west, so his father sent him to a psychiatrist to make sure the witnessing of the accident had no serious psychological repercussions. The boy visited the psychiatrist four times and then the doctor asked Morton Toddman to please come see him. Mort was assured that his son had handled the tragedy admirably, that there were no scars. Morton got up to leave, ready to take Eugene from the waiting room, when the doctor coughed. Significantly.

"Doctor?"

The doctor cleared his throat again and puffed twice on his pipe.

"Something?" Mort asked.

"Mr. Toddman," the psychiatrist said, "has Eugene discussed the incident with you?"

"No. Not really. Not in great depth. Not yet."

"I told you that your son came through this experience remarkably well. He's a very intelligent boy. Quite sensitive, perceptive. I believe that we did some very serious and rather remarkable probing into your son's emotional make-up."

"Good."

"*Very* good. I felt there were no barriers, no facades between us during our discussions."

"I'm glad."

The doctor nodded. "Eugene invited the little girl to the pond. He led her, more or less, to the spot where she fell through the ice. I assure you I am aware of the shock factor and the speed with which such tragedies occur, but . . . Eugene made no effort to save her from death. In some sense, certainly psychologically, your son can be said to be *responsible* for her death."

"It was an accident," said Mort.

"Yes, yes, of course. All I mean is that it would be normal if Eugene *felt* responsible. Harbored strong sensations of guilt or fear or . . ." the doctor waved his hand. "That would be quite normal."

"And?"

"And he doesn't. Hasn't. And won't, probably." The doctor sighed. "Mr. Toddman. Eugene has suffered through an incredibly traumatic experience. I absolutely do not feel as if he is repressing anything, and yet . . . I can discern no emotional reaction other than . . . other than curiosity. In no way am I able to judge, evaluate, predict the results of this . . . accident."

Mort stood up.

"Mr. Toddman. I cannot say that I think further treatment would be beneficial or even advisable. Frankly, I don't think it would be anything but a waste of your money. But I do suggest . . ." Here the doctor put his pipe down and spun his leather chair around to face the window. ". . . I do suggest . . . you watch out for the kid." He turned back to Mort and shrugged.

"Thanks, doc," said Morton Toddman.

Mort retrieved Eugene, and as they rode home, Mort's arm slipped around his son's shoulder. He kept his whole hand on the top of Eugene's head, gently massaging with his fingers. Eugene felt comforting chills run up and down his spine, spread into his cheeks, and then through the rest of his body. They said practically nothing the whole ride back. Stopped for a hot chocolate about halfway, and then, when they were back in the car, Mort turned on the radio. Then he turned it off. "You okay?" Mort asked quietly.

Eugene nodded and felt good. He moved over to lean against his father.

"Joanie's parents would like to talk with you. They called."

"What for?"

"Ohhh. I guess they just want you to give 'em a few extra memories."

"Should I?"

"Why not?"

Eugene shrugged.

"You know, Gene, I'm a writer. Not an important one, particularly, but still . . . a lot of my . . . my *communicating* is my writing. That's what my emotion goes into and when I feel and when I think, it winds up on paper. Unfortunately, I don't always have much left over for . . . what counts. But I'm older than you and maybe know some things that you just can't quite know yet. I can use my age and my experience to give you a tip."

Mort drove for about a quarter of a mile without speaking. Then he looked back at his son.

"Do your best to deal with people, Gene. Respect what they have to offer. Take what they want to give and don't make unreasonable demands. And give them what they want because it's really no big deal. Do you understand what I mean?"

"I guess so. I dunno. It doesn't sound like much fun."

Eugene saw his father's thoughtful expression and touched Mort's leg affectionately. He glanced out at the highway scenery and the telephone poles rushing by them, and rolled up the car window, sealing himself in. Eugene felt safe.

Back at school, Eugene took up interest, again, in his schoolwork. He read *Gone With the Wind* and made a water wheel. His fellow sixth-graders constantly asked him about the incident, and, once again, as with the jagged slash on his wrist, Eugene was the center of attention. He answered everyone's questions about Joanie's death. Classmates, teachers, family, Joanie's parents—they all wanted to know how he felt—how he thought. They all wanted him to tell. So he thought about his friend and how he had liked her. He heard her screams of terror while she was alive and struggling. He thought of how odd she had looked pressed up under the ice; how still and calm and yet how . . . confused. He conjured up that moment of never-before-felt excruciating pleasure. And the pain that followed. And the moment when he could swallow and feel nothing.

He soon wearied of the repetitiveness of it all and couldn't wait to move out to L.A.

3.

For the young, the naive, the impressionable, the rich, and the fearful, Beverly Hills is a paradise.

Eugene loved it.

There is no sense of reality to Beverly Hills, to the city or to the people. The weather lulls the residents into believing that the world is a sunny afternoon with only a thin layer of smog to prevent perfection. The only disturbing sounds, while lying by the pool, are the dull thuds of finely placed tennis balls. The only poor people are maids. And they aren't around long enough to become offensive—every few weeks, the police round up the Mexicans and South Americans loitering by the Beverly Hills Hotel bus stop and send them all back south of the border. No one works for a living, if casual conversations are to be believed. Salesmen say they're actors. Surfers say they're actors. Druggists and students and sixty-year-old extras say they're actors. Actors eventually have to say they're real estate agents or, if successful enough, stay home at private screenings so they

don't have to say anything. Mouths in cafés on Sunset
Boulevard open against a background of tanned skin and
sunglasses to talk show biz. There are more spinach salad
and Marguerita luncheon specials than anywhere in the world.

Green is the magic color. Money and manicured lawns are
the two most visible components, and Eugene ate it all up
right from the start. He saw beauty everywhere he looked.
The people, their clothes, their homes were all beautiful.
Everything inside their homes, everything outside. The views.
Even the open spaces between objects. All beautiful. Somehow, even *nothing* has the feel of shaped elegance. Beverly
Hills is the perfection of cosmetic pulchritude, transient
wealth, and the ultimate architectural and philosophical triumph
of form over content. The Toddmans did their best to blend
right in.

Morton Toddman's new house was spectacular. On top of a
mountain overlooking the city, the house had its pool and
tennis court. Soon it had a gardener, a pool-man, a maid, a
butler, hangers-on, and it soon had lots of parties going on
within it. Mort got the hang of Southern California living
very quickly—he became a great party-giver. At his soirées,
there would be musicians who would grace the gathering
and tickle those ivories or strum them strings. Liquor flowed
freely, food was always superbly prepared, and the atmo-
sphere was never one of anything but casual fun. Barbra
Streisand once sang in Eugene's living room before she was
very famous. Milton Berle once had too much to drink and
threw up on Eugene's turtle.

Eugene attended all of his father's parties. Dressed up in
spiffy casual outfits, hair well groomed, serving drinks and
hors d'oeuvres, changing the jazz records on the turntable,
he made the guests laugh with his precocious humor and
childlike half-grasp of sophistication. As he grew older and
his presence became more commanding, he found out he
was witty and charming. At twelve and a half he could light
women's cigarettes very smoothly, at thirteen could toss
around a French phrase or two to flatter an unattended-to
wife. Constantly surrounded by firm-breasted women wearing low-cut gowns or unbuttoned shirts, long-legged women

wearing tight shorts, tennis skirts, or skimpy bathing suits, beautiful women making ringlets with his hair or fixing his untucked shirt, Eugene, without really knowing his motives or the possible results, began to lust. Not after anything specific, but, befitting his youth, after almost anything he could think of. As the parties grew more frequent and the surrounding pleasures more numerous, his desire became insatiable, with no viable outlet, no channel toward success. He longed for money, having a vague inkling that money had something to do with satisfying one's lust. He became finicky about his clothes, instinctively knowing what was appealing and what was too much or too little. He suddenly was all too conscious of his body—painfully aware of its length and scrawniness. Blue balls, agonizingly, came and went. Chest and pubic hair sprouted. Dreaded blackheads and pimples and beloved shaving cuts occasionally marred his features. His eyes were already beginning to form into what would become his greatest physical asset and his greatest communicative drawback. Already, it was possible to peer into them and see arrogance and awareness and curiosity all at once. His eyes lusted. He smiled with his eyes. They were eyes that were incapable of lying, even then—a trait that endeared him to some and disgusted others.

Eugene had bedroom eyes before he knew what to do in a bedroom.

In his new L.A. school, Eugene hadn't attained the popularity of his earlier days, although his sense of humor and smooth assurance always kept people interested in him. He made no effort to make new friends, and his junior-high peers took his aloofness as a kind of passive arrogance and disinterest, which was exactly right. Becoming preoccupied with what he considered essential—the fulfillment of his vague desires —Eugene became disinterested in the nonessential. The concrete sciences now struck him as faintly ridiculous; it bored him to pursue anything that had one specific solution, that could be borne out by systematic logic. It was much more entertaining to go after what had *many* solutions . . . or none. He still read voraciously, but had little interest in reading, for the most part, what was assigned to him in school. His schoolwork suffered and a pattern was being forged. Eugene conquered what interested him—and what didn't interest him was allowed to pass by untouched.

He had always been a natural athlete, graceful and steady, strong and assured. Most importantly, he'd always had the eyes of an athlete, the eyes that let him follow the path of a well-hit fly ball or judge the distance between a wide receiver and the appointed spot for a game-winning catch. Now, athletics began to bore him—the physical satisfaction left him unfulfilled, hollow—and his lack of athletic participation began to cut him off from the popular jock crowd, those who played endless numbers of games of half-court three-on-three during each lunch hour. The Dodgers were in L.A. now and the town was in love with Duke Snider. The one constant in Eugene's life was still Willie Mays, and the idolized Willie was not a beloved figure to Dodger fans. Mays, now entering his prime, was poetry on the diamond. Eugene could not understand Los Angeles' lack of appreciation for this human god. Territorial loyalty had nothing to do with Eugene's devotion to Willie—it was blind love for perfection. And it baffled him that anyone could feel otherwise.

All around Eugene kids were going steady, trotting off to dances, smoking cigarettes, and making out. Eugene didn't see anyone he wanted to go steady with, he didn't like the taste of tobacco, and making out struck him as vaguely unsatisfying. Like playing a game where there could be no winner. Girls usually either giggled at the serious parts or took the whole thing *so* seriously that it became uncomfortable. Their heads would roll back, strange noises would come sighing or panting out of their mouths, their eyes would gloss over with a strange puppy-like glaze of love, power, contentment, excitement, and fear. In these situations, Eugene was usually left with a respectable hard-on and the evening's end would find him in the bathroom behind carefully locked doors, moaning and writhing on the shag carpet with a couple of old copies of *Playboy*.

Which left dancing.

And dancing was something else again.

There was a six-month span when, as far as Eugene could tell, all of Beverly Hills got Bar-Mitzvahed and Eugene was going to party after party. He had never had any religious training. Mort being a confirmed atheist, it was easy for Eugene never to interest himself in the questions of what made man like he was. Besides, he was too absorbed in *being* like he was. His mother had been a Protestant, that he knew. And Mort was a Jew, but was tied to Judaism basically only by his eating habits—Sunday-morning lox and bagels and a taste for dry, almost stale pound cake. So now, putting in his first appearances in temple, Eugene was astonished. Listening to gibberish, wearing silly, round hats, having to spend time talking to overdone, oversprayed hairstyles, expensive gaudy jewelry, and loud madras sportjackets; standing in the heat as his friends proclaimed their manhood in high-pitched puberty-ridden voices—Eugene was amazed at the wealth, the tastelessness, the competition, the ridiculous pride in the absurd, the strength drawn from the past, the cliquish and unreal ethnic celebratory hubris. But it was all worth it because there would then be a party where Eugene could twist his life away.

On the dance floor he was dynamite.

He would casually saunter over to whatever girl appealed to him, suggest a stroll toward the bandstand, wait for the music to start, and then hips would gyrate, feet fly, and legs strut. Eventually, hair wet and falling over his forehead, the sportcoat would come off and be casually slung over a shoulder, the tie would loosen, white shirt sleeves would crumple up to the forearms, Coke, with desperately needed ice, was sipped. Eugene would grin gleefully as the music pounded on and he bopped around, sliding across the country club or restaurant or synagogue. Morton Toddman would come late at night and pick up his son, driving the bopper home. Eugene would stand in front of a mirror in his room, posing and grinning at himself, looking cool, breathing hard; then he would dive into the swimming pool, naked, and swim up above the twinkling lights of the San Fernando Valley.

By fourteen, growing problems had nearly ended—no more sudden testicle pains, no more wet dreams—and the teenager could feel his physical pains diminishing. Fourteen brought on his first spurt of complex thoughts, confusing observations, puzzling mental awarenesses. His voice changed, and so, too, did his view of the world. He developed his first inkling that external forces were slowly nibbling away at his self-preoccupation. He read J. D. Salinger.

At his father's parties, though, Eugene shied away from conversation that tended toward any intellectual weightiness. Clogging up his living room were so many intelligent, successful people. The intelligent people all said different things, all expounded different philosophies, all spewed out different solutions and advocated different systems. The successful people all had money and nice clothes. They could all get tickets to the good sports events and they could all afford to have electrically operated garage doors and heated swimming pools.

The intelligent people all thought differently and the successful people all acted the same.

No one seemed too happy with his present situation. Resignation ricocheted from adult to adult. Their heads bent down dejectedly when mentioning a membership in a new private club; their faces lit up when it came to tales of sneaking into Ebbett's field. Everyone talked about the old days as if the combination of poverty and youth was the key to good times. Eugene observed, amidst the combination of middle age and wealth, unhappy marriages, adultery, homosexuality.

"Women are all unhappy," Eugene heard an interior decorator announce.

"Aren't we all, dear," was said by his companion, a tanned, wavy-haired smiler.

The people he observed at close range strove desperately to attain things they hated, as if afraid to possess what they loved, terrified not to possess at all. They were neither content nor fulfilled, but still, miraculously, they turned out situation comedy after situation comedy and never failed to laugh when they got drunk or won a big tennis game. Eugene *liked* these people. They were all *nice*—just terribly *fragile*—and they all had to be handled delicately. And delicacy does not involve truth. So Eugene either had to lie or withdraw as he dealt with people. He either had to alienate or hide behind a mask of compassion and understanding. Several times, in the middle of an intense discussion—of politics, worldly affairs, true personal thoughts and insights—with his father's friends, Eugene would develop this horrid smirk on his face, this dreadful smile that he couldn't wipe clean. He began to comprehend how little communication there was underneath *words*. Language became, to him, as he thought it seemed to be to all others, a means of avoiding reality, a way to sidestep truth. A way to hide and to hurt and to use and to lie.

Eugene wondered whether it was people's words or people's thoughts that had become impossible for him to take seriously.

But soon Eugene Toddman, his mind advancing rapidly, was able to file away the perceptions he wanted to save and reject the impressions that left him cold. Images flickered by, sparking new thoughts and remembrances of old thoughts. Eugene was learning not only how to participate in the world's movements, but how to observe them. People settled for *means* instead of *ends,* and idealistic young Eugene decided not to settle. He had finally found a worthy object on which to concentrate his lust. He now knew what he wanted—the culmination of all his observations, frustrations, and desires:

Eugene wanted Sandra Ragnow, who was thirty-seven years old, wore low-cut dresses, had hard, sexy thighs, drank like a fish, and was married to the producer of two of the last three Academy Award–winning films.

4.

Eugene was not alone in his craving for Sandra Ragnow.
Every man who knew her probably, at one time or another,
wanted to cut a slice of her hair pie.

But Eugene wanted her so *badly*. He thought about her
constantly, ached for her, wanted to *devour* her.

He, of course, had no chance.

Sexy thirty-seven-year-old women rarely put out for horny
fourteen-year-old boys. But Eugene, from fourteen till sixteen, got many a night of masturbatory fantasy from Sandra.
She kept that shag-carpet odor in his nostrils for years to
come. And that was something to be thankful for.

The fifties had ended, and a lot of people *everywhere* had
things to be thankful for. Logic appeared to be floating
timidly through the air. The country was well protected.
Things were changing, but for the first time in a long while,
change seemed secure and natural. People were not particu-

larly afraid of the future and seemed satisfied with the present.

Morton Toddman was riding the crest of the wave of prosperity. His first television venture was a smash, his second was a bigger smash. And Morton's son got to observe, firsthand, that, somehow, when someone makes a lot of money doing something he's good at, people feel that his competence spreads into other fields. Thus, Morton was approached by and got involved with the behind-the-scenes world of Democratic politics. He raised a lot of cash, wrote a few speeches, got to know senators and governors and cabinet members. He got richer. And safer. And even richer.

As security enveloped *his* world, Eugene's sense of detachment was growing. He had a solid group of friends. He had fun and his worries were at a minimum. But he curiously found himself in a state of informal isolation.

Eugene could not get concerned over whether French homework was completed on time or not. He did not care if he was caught cutting class to go to the beach. He stayed away from his high-school football games and basketball games and he did not like having to go to a movie with a girl, unobtrusively putting his arm around her, then humbly having to ask for a kiss goodnight. Arguing politics did nothing for him. He didn't get along with conservatives, liberals, or radicals, resisting anyone who tried to fit him into any sort of pattern. His teachers told him he was very intelligent and that he should get straight As—so he stopped working and just got by. His friends said they admired him for staying clear of the in-crowd—so Eugene immediately wooed and won the most popular girl in his grade, went out with her to every social gathering for a month, developed a new popularity, and then dropped her cold. He read poetry and dressed hip till the hipsters embraced him, then he started wearing expensive well-fitting clothes and reading nothing but detective novels. At nights, in his bathroom or under his covers, Eugene gloriously imagined Sandra Ragnow blowing him while he covered her in chocolate syrup. She sat on his face for days on end, he licked every pore in her body, performed every obscene act imaginable. He'd be held down by two naked women while she walked all over him. *She* was held down while he jerked off on her tits. Threesomes, foursomes, and upwards—doing it in bed, on the floor, in a closet or a bathtub. The two or three times a month Eugene actually saw Sandra, he would exchange pleasantries, smile slyly at her, get a boner, and saunter off.

He basked in the L.A. sun and floated in his pool. He sometimes said the wrong thing, thinking he was smarter than he really was. He usually said the right thing, being brighter than he *really* thought he was. He was funny. Intuitive. He *knew* things. His eyes shone.

In his spare time, Eugene started to write.

And Morton *stopped* writing. He was now a studio executive, and though still in love with words and thought, he settled for financial independence and a steady flow of women. And there was a flow—success does have its groupies. Actresses hot for roles, starstruck tourists hot for celebrity-gazing, plain cunt hot for money, fame, and sometimes on that rare occasion, even for flesh. Mort was often irked about the fact that no one was particularly hot for what he considered his *self*, and this often made him restless and dissatisfied. And resentful. He didn't treat his women too well—he didn't like them, got no enjoyment from them. For all of his participation, Mort got no true pleasure out of sex. He liked orgasms and all that, and could understand the thrill that a good female body could give, but there was no real appreciation. No true grasp of beauty, no more feel for the emotion hiding behind the physicality of a relationship. Mort's women were more for show. If a girl was tall, blonde, and swallowed it, she met Mort's requirements. Everyone was envious of his string of conquests—and he liked the image. Being the recipient of other people's envy somehow eased Mort's loneliness. And besides, Eugene loved them all. The junior Toddman got to pat suntan lotion on delicate shoulder blades and eat pastrami sandwiches under the gaze of round, brown eyes. Many were actresses, so Eugene got to watch TV with his friends and point out women who'd kissed him on the cheek or put ice on a sprained ankle. Some were businesswomen, some were secretaries. One was his orthodontist's nurse, and she would rub her incredible breasts against his chest while she took molds of his overbite—a little bribe to keep him quiet. Mort liked, needed, the turnover. He never had to expose himself too deeply, his mind was rarely probed. In fact, Mort's mind rarely had to function at all, anymore.

He started drinking fairly heavily.

And he began swimming late at night.

Mort would sit out by the pool at two or three in the morning. First, he would think. He would think about how, his whole life, he had done exactly what he had wanted to do. He lived where he wanted, he lived the way he wanted. Mort would sit out by the pool and wonder how he could have lived the life he'd always wanted and still be so miserable. Then he would sit some more, trail his finger through the seventy-eight-degree water, and search for excuses to avoid facing his thoughts.

When Mort turned forty, he began to miss his dead wife terribly. He particularly missed her bathrobe. She used to wear this quilted robe, wore it for several years. She would hang it on the back of their closet door, and whenever Mort opened the closet he could get a faint whiff of the robe, a faint whiff of his wife. With the smell came, always, a conjuring up of her taste and her feel. Her smoothness and that unmistakable, always distinct taste of lips and tongue. In L.A., when Mort thought about his wife, he always thought about her robe. How it had smelled like her, how he used to keep his hands on it to stay warm, how comfortable she looked in it. Sometimes Mort would awake in the middle of the night, wanting nothing more than his wife, in her robe, next to him with a Sunday *Times* crossword puzzle. He felt like he should reach over and try to touch her but would, instead, turn on the bedside lamp and attempt to read himself to sleep. Mort grew more and more melancholy, became richer and richer, slept with woman after woman. Started to eat constantly as well as drink. He grew paunchy. Shapeless. Mort was unhappy.

Eugene was too busy to be unhappy.

It hadn't taken long for disruption to settle into the sixties, and Eugene was glad to plunge into the turmoil. The politics of sophistication and youth proved as ineffective and unintelligent as any other politics. The cold war was freezing its ass off, people began to get nervous again about the atom bomb, negroes began to bother everyone, demanding equality. Everybody had a cause, everyone developed integrity. People's backbones suddenly straightened up with moral fiber and righteous indignation.

In 1962, Eugene was fifteen years old, a grade ahead of where he should have been, vehemently concerned about the civil rights movement, an admirer of Malcolm X, a devotee of Lenny Bruce, a constant attender of Bergman and Fellini films. He was hip. Cool. He believed in free speech and free thinking and free action. His beliefs were truthful, decent, and instinctive—and were temporary diversions only. Everything Eugene believed was an attempt to escape from what was slowly becoming a bewilderingly nagging sense of boredom, emptiness, and dissatisfaction. He couldn't place it, couldn't define it. Most of the time he wasn't even aware of it. But the more dissatisfied he became, the more passionately he chased after beliefs. Waiting to escape the trappings of youth and the times, and the frustrating confines of his surroundings, Eugene sprouted and nurtured his first scraggly moustache.

He dated. And now he had more freedom and later hours in which to score. But fifteen-year-old girls were not yet, on the whole, fucking, and older women were not, on the whole, fucking fifteen-year-old boys. Eugene's first love, Sandra Ragnow, was still around—but a beat-off queen no longer. Alcohol had begun to puff out her face, her breasts had sagged a bit, and lines rippled in her arms and neck. The changes were barely noticeable to the unscrutinizing eye. But to Eugene the damage was, though certainly not complete, now inevitable. If given the chance, Eugene still would have jumped on top of her, but time had diminished the ideal.

One ideal still thankfully timeless was Willie Mays. Eugene eagerly checked the box score every morning to follow

Number Twenty-Four's glory. Finally accepted by California, Willie was performing daily miracles and was leading the Giants to a pennant, having perhaps his greatest season. Eugene managed to catch a few Giant-Dodger games—and had the extra satisfaction of alienating Dodger fans in box seats all around him. Willie had opened the season with a home run and he kept on pounding homers and stealing bases all year. Nineteen sixty-two ended on a satisfying note—Mays took the Giants through the seventh game of the World Series against the Yanks, and if it hadn't been for Bobby Richardson's lucky positioning, would have taken them all the way. He would have. All the *way!*

In 1963, Eugene turned sixteen and the images that were his youth were speeding by. At sixteen Eugene was given a new car, graduated from high school, got laid at last, and went off to Europe for the summer.

His high-school graduation was anticlimactic. Eugene had needed an A on his biology final to pass the class. He easily pulled off the A, was picked to be one of three students to deliver a graduation-night speech, and then decided not to attend the ceremony. That night, he went to a party at a friend's house, stuck around for a while, and said his farewells to a large group of peripheral pals. Everyone was laughing and crying and signing each other's yearbooks and getting all excited. Eugene knew he'd see the people he cared about and he didn't really care about the people he wouldn't see. So he left early and met up with another group. Eugene and his best friend, Casey, drank a lot of beer—they got a stranger at a liquor store to buy it for them—and left once again to make the rounds and see a few girls. They both felt good and relaxed; it was fun driving the L.A. freeways drinking beer. Someone had the use of a boat, so Eugene and Casey and a few other people wound up sailing at midnight. They floated around the marina till almost dawn, drank, smoked cigarettes, and two or three people threw up. They discussed their future plans, got philosophical as only drunken teen-agers can on a night of uncertainty and importance.

"I can't believe it. I can't believe we're through," one philosopher kept repeating over and over again.

"Try to believe it," Eugene told him.

"Do you have a cigarette?" a girl asked. Eugene shook his head and the girl tucked one leg under another and said "Jeezuz H. Christ."

Another girl was giggling hysterically watching her boy-friend penning a puppet's face on his thumb and forefinger.

Eugene stepped out of the cabin, walked to the far end of the boat. He trailed his hand through the cold water, skimmed his palm over the choppy waves. He blinked. Then yawned.

He tried to focus on the stars, gave up when his head started to spin. He slid onto the floor, laughing quietly to himself. He stared at the tilting mast, felt himself toughen up, put a sneer on his face, banged his fist into his open hand. He felt like getting into a fight, like hitting someone, or getting hit. He rubbed his jaw, imagining a trickle of blood coming down off his lip. And suddenly, he straightened up and threw a left, then a right and an uppercut and it was all over. He smiled, the victor, and turned around and was in the middle of a championship basketball game. Three . . . two . . . one . . . and he jumped from thirty feet out and his body hung up perfectly and the ball swished through the hoop at the buzzer. Pandemonium. Hysterics. And before the crowd could even carry him out of the arena on its shoulders, his mind really stretched now and took him to a king's palace in the Mideast. Dancing girls, a harem. Diamonds and soft fur rugs. A beautiful veiled brunette was feeding him grapes, pouring his wine, kissing him, touching him.

Eugene rubbed a hand over his muscle, dragged a mani-cured nail over the straining bulge. He wondered what he was going to do, wondered what was going to happen to his life, wished he knew what accolades and awards he'd re-ceive, what havoc and destruction he would wreak. Eugene threw a quick jab at the sea and rubbed some sweat off his forehead. He stood up, ready to battle the mightiest forces of the universe.

"Close the door, dickhead!" Casey yelled out.

Eugene got home as the sun was coming up, his eyes drooping and his mind clouded. The Toddmans' maid, just getting going for the day, chided Eugene for coming home so late and for being drunk. He smiled and shrugged and she squeezed him a glass of fresh orange juice. Eugene took the glass, walked out back to catch the morn. He saw Morton sitting by the pool, staring vacantly out over L.A. Deciding not to disturb his father, Eugene went upstairs and collapsed on his bed, dreaming of beer and the future and milk-white thighs.

The next night, Morton threw his own party to celebrate Eugene's graduation. The crowd came—Eugene was still a popular kid; he still charmed 'em. People played tennis under the lights. It was warm enough to go swimming. Eugene told everyone about his college plans, his upcoming trip to Europe, his various girlfriends. Sandra was there, drunk and wandering from clique to clique. She looked bad. Old. Old and tired and used. Her skin had somehow dried up and gotten crinkly. Sandra was separated from her husband and was available now. She moved around *making* herself available as Eugene watched her sadly. He caught her eye once or twice and simply stared through her, trying to see into her decline. Sandra smiled at him, straightened her bathing suit.

Around midnight, one of the women at the party got too drunk and began to abuse another guest. She was helped upstairs to Eugene's room, and she told Eugene to check on her in half an hour. The party was starting to thin out, people were congratulating the graduate, thanking Mort, and leaving. Mort came over to his son. He tousled Eugene's hair and they had their serious talk.

"You should be proud."

Eugene didn't answer. Looked down at his shoes.

"*Are* you proud?"

"No." Eugene shrugged.

A smile and, "Why not?"

Eugene shook his head and said, "I don't know." His hand twisted to show that he *didn't* know. They looked at each other. Behind them, two glasses clinked together. "Why do *you* sit out at the pool all night?"

"*I* don't know."

Mort looked at his son, saw a tall, skinny, sort of good-looking son with curious eyes.

"I *know,* Gene." Mort yawned, really more of a sigh. "I sit up all night because I'm looking for something I can't have."

"What?"

"Youth." Mort smiled again. "Age turns men into clichés, Gene. A man turns out to be just like every other man."

"Maybe that's why I'm not proud."

They kissed. Mort said goodbye to the last guest and took his date back to her home and two small children. Eugene went upstairs to check on the drunken woman in his room. She was naked under the covers of Eugene's bed, and not really so liquored up anymore. It took her fifteen minutes to seduce him, drawing him down clumsily on top of her. Eventually, Eugene got the hang of it. He sucked and grabbed whatever got in his way, came three times in twenty minutes, babbled about love and a great body, lay gasping. Then silent.

Eugene was stunned that anything could be so much *fun*.

And when they were both, finally, physically exhausted, hot and dripping wet, Eugene said, "You know. This is the first time I've ever had a woman in my room."

"Sorry to break your string."

"Ahhhh," said Eugene, "for you I'd break the habits of a lifetime."

And when Patty, the woman, stood over his bed struggling to pull herself back into her dress, Eugene sat back with a satisfied smirk on his face thinking how much fun it was, how great it was, how much *fun*. His eyes glowed with pleasure and pride and a sense of well-being that added to his excitement. He relived it, reexperienced it, felt it all over again. And after Patty left he stayed awake for a while, his face practically swaggering until he finally just had to hop out of bed and laugh out loud, swing his fist under the watchful eye of his autographed picture of Willie Mays, and let out a whoop. From somewhere downstairs, a dog barked and a screendoor blew shut.

Two days later, Eugene left for Europe.

5.

A letter from Eugene Toddman to Lisa Gerner, a high-school girlfriend:

September 2, 1963

Sweet Lucille,

Don't panic. I realize it's been quite a while since you've heard from me, but I haven't really forgotten your name. I've just always wanted to call someone Sweet Lucille.

Uh . . . heh heh heh . . . you may have wondered why you haven't heard from me in nearly three months. Especially since I vaguely recall something about promising to write every day. Ah, the rash promises of youth. Not to mention the promised rash of youth. Okay. Sorry. Don't mean to be frivolous.

I haven't written because I've been living.

I fear this may sound a bit pretentious. It is, but it's also true. Europe has been a fantasy come true for me. I have been to

England, France, Germany, Sweden, Italy, Denmark, and Holland and I have learned to guzzle heavy alcohol and gently sip liqueurs; have stuffed my face with undreamed-of delicacies; have gaped at great art; have met wonderful people who bought me drinks and took me places and showed me easy friendship; and I have gotten laid in every country except Sweden.

Excuse my crudeness, S.L. (that's for Sweet Lucille, remember?). But every time I got laid (NOTE: for three months that's eight different women, and—oh, the thrill of it all!—I'm not sure exactly how many times!)—every time I got laid, I thought, ''Jesus Fucking Christ, am I glad I'm not in the back seat of a Camaro trying to get Lisa Gerner's bra off.'' I mean no disrespect. It's what I thought. It's what I'm thinking. It's why I haven't written—partially. The other part is that it would have pained me to stop looking or walking or drinking or anything to take pen in hand and try to describe what I was doing, what I was thinking. I could, I'm sure, write you a beautiful description of what it's like on a sleeper rolling through the Swiss Alps. Or describe the canals of Amsterdam or the castles of the English countryside. I could pour forth soul-searching passages filled with beauty and despair. Why would I bother, though? Why would you bother to read it? Why would you bother to read *this?* Well, I'm coming home in two days, so I suppose I'll find out then, when I see how you respond to this wonderfully carefree epistle.

I haven't seen you in three months and I have seen so much else during that time. I forget if you understand what I think and the way I see. I forget if you have any sense of humor. Will you make love to me and wake me up with croissants and espresso? I will settle for some Metrecal and Sanka, I think, as long as the making-love part is still there.

Why am I writing this letter? Even more important, why am I *mailing* this letter? I am drunk in a Paris café, true, but alcohol is not an excuse. It is a near necessity. Oh *yes!* Fitzgerald, Hemingway, Miller, and Toddman.

I look forward to seeing you. I hate the thought of returning from paradise. Although it'll be good to know what Willie's hitting every day.

I am growing up. Thank God I'm rich.

Love,

Eugene "Meursault" Toddman

P.S.   I have also managed to hit a few museums and see a few
sights. Tate Gallery is amazing. Skansen (Deer Park) in
Stockholm a thing of joy. Italian drivers crazy. Michelangelo's *David* is probably the greatest thing I've ever seen
in my entire life. Paris has snared me. I hope to return
one day and spend months getting sucked in by it. Everywhere I turn, there seems to be a doorway leading me to
some new paradise. Try French fries with mayonnaise.

6.

Eugene came back from Europe and immediately went off to Berkeley to begin his college career. He stepped off the plane at the Oakland airport, took a cab to Bowles Hall, his new home, and looked over toward the campus to glimpse the towering point of the Campanile, showing the way toward the heavens *and* giving the exact hour of the day, both at the same time.

Berkeley was a new life for Eugene. He knew no one there except Casey—the two good friends decided to stick together a little longer—so, for the most part, he was forced to create himself for others once again.

Eugene's first quarter was a memorable one. The university taught him in a Psych 12 course that people are motivated by pleasure—they let this startling piece of information soak in by having a rat demonstrate his willingness to scramble over a wall to reach a piece of cheese. In Philosophy 2, Eugene was surprised to learn that Plato was a fascist. He managed to learn a little bit about the Trojan War (and

Agamemnon dead) and a little bit about American History (The question is, said Thoreau, what are you doing out *there?*) and a little bit about how to eat runny dorm eggs and make his own coffee. Student poets in a creative writing course taught him that we all want to return to the womb. His first paper topic was "Explain why Seymour Glass committed suicide." He didn't really know.

Eugene discovered that there were depths to literature he never knew existed. He began to perceive that there were levels to life he had never suspected. Eugene learned a little bit about human beings.

He'd never had an affinity for the foibles of people around him, still, he'd always been around people he liked, so he just assumed that he liked people. As with his early generalized lust, Eugene's concept of friendship was to appreciate everyone, except Casey, from a distance. As his sensual censors became more sophisticated, so did he begin to discriminate mentally. He began to realize there were people he *didn't* like. This came as quite a shock, and Eugene tried to fight it, tried to like everyone. Which is an impossibility when living in a college dorm.

In Eugene's dorm there was a short fat guy with a handlebar moustache who used to dress up and go to the opera by himself. He lived with a guy who showed Eugene, in great confidence, his collection of fingernail and toenail clippings that he'd saved up for seven years. There was a muscle-bound behemoth who refused to get undressed in front of his angelfish. Right next to Eugene was a religious fanatic who loved only two things—Jesus and playing the trombone at five in the morning. There were naive virgins who spent twenty-four hours a day lying about the tail they had managed to dip into, and there were apelike jocks who liked nothing better than snapping their towels at bare asses in the bathroom. There were Chinese people who didn't do anything but sit in their rooms and do complex math equations, low-riders with girlfriends who used the men's showers, musicians and alcoholics and homosexuals and a couple of people whose doors were always closed and nobody had any idea who the hell they were. It was your typical dorm crew, and Eugene smiled bravely through the wrestling matches on the dinner tables and the water-balloon fights in the hallway. He definitely threw more than his share of frisbees.

Around the end of November, Eugene stepped out of the elevator that had dirty slogans painted all over it and started to walk down the hallway toward his cubicle. He passed the lounge and a television set was blaring, a crowd of people hunched around it. Everyone was very quiet. Kennedy had been shot.

Eugene remembered, when he was very young, the look on his father's face when Bobby Thompson hit his pennant-winning home run. Mort had sat stunned, motionless, for a ten-second eternity. Then he exploded, jumped up, his arms waving, flapping his legs, rubbery, dancing out in all directions. He laughed and yelled and kissed Eugene over and over again. Now, as Mort's son peered into the room with the television set, he saw the same shared confusion, that shocking awareness of actual observation and participation in a moment of personal and historical upheaval. Eugene waited, expecting the past to repeat itself, waiting for the silence to turn to frenzied, gleeful acceptance. Instead, all eyes turned to him, as if hoping this new face would deny what they had just witnessed. Needless to say, they turned to the wrong person.

Down the hall, someone laughed. Eugene walked eight more steps into his own room and turned on his own TV. He watched as Kennedy was shot six more times on instant replay. It was on all the channels, every radio station—a solemn hum buzzing through the airwaves and burning into people's consciousness. Eugene flicked off the set. He stepped out into the hallway, threw a small rubber ball against the ceiling, bouncing it off the wall a few times. Almost everyone was watching the news. A few people were already getting bored. The trombone player was crying. The fat boy was listening to Rigoletto on his headphones. Some stayed busy venting their anger and frustration. Some consoled others. Eugene surveyed the hallway, turned to the window and looked out. People were bent with sorrow, stooped with outrage and confusion. They looked like grief-stricken ants milling around looking for something to do.

And all this clicked, all this flashed, all this froze for Eugene along with one thought: Things are just like always, only sadder.

Time passed.

Eugene became selective about the company he kept.

He tried to stay away from the assholes.

He and Casey started going into San Francisco a lot. Caught a decent amount of jazz. Sat and drank espresso at Enrico's and would usually go into Ann's 44 (thanks to fake IDs) where Lenny Bruce still sometimes hung around. They'd go into the City Lights Bookstore just to browse, talking with people about the scene they were a few years too late to really catch.

Eugene appreciated Casey's friendship. Words weren't necessary, just a dart of an eye, and they could make each other laugh or let the other one know that someone had said something idiotic, or could even pinpoint the perpetrator of a major fart in a crowded elevator. They drank the same drink and had the same sense of humor. They both thought sex was dirty and they both preferred it that way. They both loved to watch football and use their stereo headphones. They liked to sit up and talk seriously or watch people go by and make fun of them. Eugene was the aggressor when it came to picking up women, Casey was the organizer if plans had to be made. Eugene could eat more pizza, Casey could throw up on command. They were pals and they were equals and they had no qualms about letting time slip away just being in each other's company.

Movies helped the hours slip by, too. Capra, Kazan, and Wilder were Eugene's new mentors. Their combination of cynicism and triumph played perfectly on his mind. Cagney and Bogart and Brando and Newman were tough guys to idolize. Eugene's favorite films were *Casablanca* and *On the Waterfront* and *It's a Wonderful Life*. He became enamored of romance and justice, keeping himself aware that they were, for the most part, celluloid creations.

Things were pretty smooth, all in all. San Francisco was a good hang-out city—it had just the right combination of unthreatening sleaze, hipness, and intellect. And the weather was usually crisp and autumny so Eugene could wear his thick turtlenecks and a light leather jacket.

He grew a beard.

School began to fade into the background. Eugene did enjoy sitting around, drinking wine, discussing Yeats and Blake and Joyce, and he developed quite a reputation as a living-room wit. When someone needed a put-down or a clever phrase or an off-the-cuff intelligent one-liner, they came to Eugene. In class, he disinterestedly mumbled facts or tried, unsuccessfully, to fit his strange outlook on life into a formula. He tried, many times, to prove what he knew to be true, and when he couldn't, when logic failed to be relevant to his brand of absurdity, he took to sloughing off logic as quickly and as often as he could. When finally confronted with art, he dismissed it. Face-to-face with the incredible harnessing of all that's powerful within the human mind to form a structured vision of horror, magnificence, despair, heroic striving, Eugene shrugged it off as an entanglement of past imaginations. He found beauty often destroyed by intellect, even when *created* by it. Conscientiously, Eugene tried to sift through the rubble, but it was difficult. And the difficult to Eugene soon became the ignored.

Women, for lack of anything even remotely more beguiling, drifted into the foreground.

Susan was Eugene's first college girlfriend. She was pretty and very nice and certainly smart enough, and after one month Eugene took to staying up nights thinking of ways to get rid of her. She lasted three months more than that because it took Eugene that long to understand that people, particularly people who are sleeping together, do not make a habit of doing things the easy way, the painless way—and that there were an awful lot of people who did not think that fucking was fun but rather something mystical and meaningful. Eugene, wise and hardened college freshman, tried to explain to Susan all about the lack of implicit morality and meaning in objective actions, but all Susan did was cry and cry and say she loved Eugene and cry some more, so Eugene held on for three months before breaking her heart.

His second girlfriend broke Eugene's heart. He wrote her cute little notes and liked nothing better than to lie in bed with her and just watch her smoke. He confided in her and was absolutely truthful with her. Then they went to a party and she went home with a guy and blew his socks off. A week later, when he saw her next, Eugene asked her why. She said that was her way of talking, she had to *do* because she couldn't *say*. Eugene shrugged and mumbled some noncommittal okay, but his eyes told her he was sad so she said, "It's too bad you're too young to cope with someone like you." Eugene went home and raged and read Camus and drank tequila and swore that he was through with women.

His third girlfriend was a redheaded virgin who was a great cook. His fourth was *Casey's* girlfriend, who didn't mind if he came too soon. By the time Eugene was on his fifth college romance, he was over his second.

He and Casey shared the bottom half of a house built in 1904. It had two fireplaces and wood-beamed ceilings and a washing machine in the backyard garage that was constantly overflowing and eating up their change. There was a sitting room that was perfect for staying up all night and talking in; it got cold and eventually shoulders needed blankets wrapped around them. They had two excellent stereos, a car, a three-A.M. radio show on KALX, a store that sold Marvel Comics and a twenty-four-hour donut shop, both right around the corner.

They both went down to L.A. for the summer. Casey got a job, Eugene didn't need one, so didn't bother. He spent his summer days on the beach playing volleyball or lying out by the side of his father's pool. He went into Westwood Village and watched what looked like thousands of beautiful

UCLA cheerleaders bounce into drugstores or malt shops or into the Hamburger Hamlet. He tried surfing and ripped up his knee on the rocks. But he met a bikinied blonde who bandaged him and told him he should iron his hair. At nights, he and Casey sometimes cruised up and down the Sunset Strip or went to hear some music or shot pool down in Venice. A lot of nights they just drove aimlessly along the Pacific Coast Highway, once even making the round-trip freeway ride to Santa Barbara and back. They eagerly dove inside each other's mind. Casey was beginning to worry about what he wanted to do with his life, and what age he should get married and when he should have kids. Eugene would shake his head and laugh disgustedly and point out some incredible piece of ass crossing the street. No bars would serve them drinks in L.A. Sometimes if they bought about twelve dollars' worth of magazines and nuts, an old liquor-store owner would sell them a bottle. They both thrived on Jack-in-the-Box tacos and Baskin-Robbins mandarin chocolate sherbet. On one drive out to Disneyland, Casey decided he'd be an architect. Eugene said maybe he'd become a private eye.

Mort was the same that summer, only a little worse. He and Eugene got along well the whole vacation; had several good chats and pleasant dinners. Eugene didn't bother to look up any old friends. He read a lot. Got a pretty decent tan, occasionally exercised. He slept late and became a Johnny Carson fan, and when the fall came around, Eugene headed up to Berkeley to settle back into his campus life. He felt the urge to try something different, to bring some brand-new stimulus into his life, Eugene was ready for some fun. He tried new classes and new friends and he wrote about forty pages of a novel. Everything he tried just missed being what he was looking for. But he kept looking. And then, wonder of wonders and joy of joys. Fireworks. Angelic harps. Choruses of angels. Hallelulah.

Eugene discovered drugs.

Casey's brother visited, bringing along a lid of flower-filled very fine marijuana. He strained it and rolled it in front of the excited and nervous Casey and Eugene, and they smoked it all night. At three A.M., Eugene wanted to know why he wasn't stoned yet. Then he settled down for the next hour to laugh hysterically at the staticky snow on television and ate two boxes of Kellogg's Sugar Frosted Flakes, six donuts, and the best peach he'd ever tasted.

Eugene stayed stoned for the rest of the year.

Marijuana was terrific and was ten bucks a lid. Hash was a true treat, and sometimes even came opiated. Both were plentiful in Berkeley, and Eugene took advantage of the seemingly endless supply.

Eugene became a hippie.

He let his hair grow long—not too many people were doing it. He wore jeans all the time and got himself some tank-top shirts. He became a frisbee expert and discovered The Dead playing in the park long before anyone. But he wasn't a *true* hippie. Even though he had a roach clip and an Indian bedspread and a black light and a mattress without a box spring for a bed. There were two things standing in the way of hippiedom. One: He couldn't stand Joan Baez. And Two: That thing which allowed him to get dressed up and drive into San Francisco for a meal or for a ballet when the mood struck. He had money, you see. And his money led him to New York for his second college summer.

Mort was back there working on some political special. He told Eugene to come on and take the summer off and visit the Museum of Modern Art and the Empire State Building and Times Square. Eugene visited. He cut his hair, shaved off his beard, got some new clothes, took advantage of the fact that Mort was loaded, and saw New York like it should be seen. With no cares, no responsibilities. And with an urgent yearning to burn a path straight to the pulse of its alluring mystique.

7.

A letter from Eugene Toddman to Casey Gruber:

June 28, 1965

Dear Fishbreath (I mean that constructively),

Heah I is in the Big Apple. Am seeing old films at the Thalia, am catching everything worth seeing on Broadway, puttering off to the ballet and I even went to an opera (Dey sang funny, dough, an' I didden like it much). I travel by cab from the Met to the Vanguard and I got very stoned at a party in the Dakota. Rough life.

Some reflections (through a bloodshot eye) of New York City:

1) There are kuh-wazy people here. Fun-loving, though. For instance, just the other day I was approached by a large negro (a total stranger, I might add) who, out of the clear blue sky, politely requested that I hand over all my money, my watch, my Captain Marvel de-coder ring, an IOU for

my first three children, and a letter of recommendation for Harvard law school. This zany local then hilariously informed me that if I didn't comply with his wacky stunt, he would bite off both of my ears.

2) Whoops. Almost forgot. In New York, one does not call negroes "negroes." We call them "niggers." There are lots of niggers and spics here. Also wops. I met this crazy fuckin' guinea down in Little Italy who I suspect is a member of the Mafia. I am suspicious only because my new pal let me know that his idea of a good joke is to take someone he doesn't like into Social Club Number 19, force-feed him 137 cannolis, and then throw him in the East River. Oh. There are way too many Jews here, too.

3) The Village is great. Hangin' around the White Horse, drinking with the ghosts of Thomas Wolfe and Dylan Thomas and a few bums and whores who occasionally pass out on the floor or throw up near my socks.

4) Good eating here in New York. No place makes pizza like this little place up on East 75th. Strange Greek food called Souvlaki. Good to eat but bad to look into. Lotta fuckin' Greeks here, too, now that I think of it.

5) Dope isn't nearly as good here as it is way out west. And it's more expensive.

That takes care of most of my observations—minorities and food and dope.

On to that most important category: Da, dada, da da da daaaahhhh . . . SEX!

New York is a very sexy city. Everyone runs around brushing up against everybody else—a lot of touching. I am constantly horny (Okay. Granted that I would be constantly horny if I lived *underwater*. No need to point that out to me in your return epic). The other day a girl bumped into me on 57th street and I got a mammoth throbber than ran up my shirt, hit me on the head, and knocked me unconscious. *That's* a sexy city, boy.

I met some twenty-eight-year-old restaurant owner who let me come in her mouth. Needless to say, I asked her if she wanted to get into a meaningful relationship. She couldn't answer, though, 'cause her mouth was full. Oh god, what a wit!!! Uh-oh. Notice

that I didn't capitalize the "g" when I wrote God. I hope no one
is looking over my shoulder.

More impressions of New York:

Dirt, heat, slime, and sleaze. Everything's a struggle, you can't
let yourself drift or slow down for a second or you get trampled.
It's *real* and even Howard Hughes couldn't walk more than a
block without seeing some amputee pissing on a building. There
are incredibly unfriendly, paranoid bastards running around hating everything. Lots of money flaunted around. Bloomingdale's
is probably the poontang capital of the world. Good drinking
city. Good walking city. I will live here someday. It's fun fun
fun.

Got to run. Hang ten for me, buddy.

      Your chum,

      Just A Latin From Manhattan

8.

Our boy returned to Berkeley satisfied; enraptured with this new view of New York. He felt vibrantly alive and was interested in feeling more.

Classes were captivating now. Eugene was learning to love to tangle with ideas—but strictly on his own terms. Ideas were still but images that stimulated a part of his consciousness. Bits and pieces of centuries of thought, selected out of context to conform to eighteen years of formless logic. He was reading a lot of good plays and English novels, studying philosophy, and he got involved with an associate professor—a thirty-year-old Marxist historian who had lovely blonde hair, long legs, and small, ballet dancer's breasts.

He read *Paradise Lost* and convinced himself that the Devil was really Milton's hero. His Philosophy 225 prof announced to the class that he was there to teach them that life was not a matter of pleasure and pain—just pain; Eugene stood up and asked if there was another professor who handled the just pleasure side. He wrote a one-act play and starred in it in two successive weekends. It was a failure. He played the guitar and formed a rock band and after three months of no jobs, they worked a wedding in the Berkeley Hills; two flower children said their own vows and wore long, flowery robes and the band was fired on the spot when Eugene insisted on playing "The Bride Cuts the Cake." Eugene wrote film criticism for the underground paper; he meditated, giving it up only when his knees started to ache at the mention of the lotus position. He fended off serious discussions of responsibility and meaning by looking cynical, patting people on the shoulder, and laughing. Everyone constantly sought his advice, always desired his company, was usually a little wary of him. There was something about his eyes, they thought. Something that made them feel uncomfortable. Something that made them suspect they were being mocked. No one ever took him seriously when he suggested picking up a couple of tickets for a night game against the Cubs at Candlestick.

Of course, there was *action,* too. No one was allowed a term of vapid thought and quiet ivory-tower life. Not with the Berkeley demonstrations.

Eugene used to have cappucino with Mario Savio and, like everyone else, was just beginning to be anti-Vietnam and anti-Johnson and anti-all-the-things-he-should-have-been-anti. But the demonstrators were mostly assholes, he thought, and Eugene knew that eventually he was going to have to risk getting clubbed over the head by a crazed policeman. He gave it his all once or twice, watched a couple of high-school kids throw a brick through a window then rush off like they were playing army, and so the next time there was a march, Eugene and Casey stole off to an Oakland bar and got drunk. Eugene stayed sympathetic and remote. Some people didn't like it, some people didn't mind. Eugene didn't really care.

He dropped mescaline for the first time. And then acid. His mind was bent and reshaped and he loved it. Lights and colors flashed, forms changed, ideas alternately struck brilliantly or were dismissed childishly. He was thrilled, he was drained. He agonized, soared to ecstatic heights, dropped to babbling lows.

It was a totally fulfilling diversion, no question about it. A personal triumph over a force that could seize control of the mind. A peek into another world. A shooting stab of absurd beauty and truth and pain. And what Eugene liked best about acid was that it went beyond words—it could not be described, only understood, only experienced. It could only be known or not known. Plus it was fun.

The year flashed by—a year of existential and psychedelic images. Mort and Eugene summered again in New York. By this time, Mort was not doing so well. He was fatter. A little cruder. And usually drunk. His women were getting a trifle older, a bit stupider. When he talked to Eugene, he still spoke affectionately and seriously, but now also usually sadly. Mort reminisced about his wife, about Lavinia. He took Eugene up to their old suburban home. While Mort rambled on about happier days, Eugene couldn't get over how small the house had become. The paint was peeling, the grass was overgrown. There were a Buick and a Mustang parked in the driveway. A lack of love was evident in the patches of weeds and the unshapely hedges. Mort and Eugene went back to the city.

Where Mort suffered and Eugene stayed intrigued. The heat was stifling, there was a garbage strike, muggings and killings and air pollution and angry people yelling at every corner. Eugene thrived. And then had to leave again.

Senior year found Eugene living with a new girlfriend and Casey and Casey's new girlfriend in a small house way up in the Berkeley hills. Eugene wore sunglasses all the time now, and smoked cigars, but he knew how funny it was, so pulled it off. Chalk up another lesson learned—know how funny you are and you can pull off almost anything.

Eugene rarely had to go to classes anymore. He was friendly with all his professors; just handed in his work to prove to them he knew his stuff and that was good enough. He read incessantly during the days. Baudelaire especially. And Pushkin. Oscar Wilde and André Breton. He read everything he could. A lot about people. Not so much history, but people aroused him. He knew everything there was to know about Hemingway and Fitzgerald and the Bloomsbury crowd and Paris in the twenties. He knew all about Tintagel and King Arthur. And how Blake threw soldiers out of his garden for interfering with the beauty.

He took long weekends with Emily (new girlfriend: strawberry-blonde hair, no sense of humor, aspiring songwriter, decent chess player, great thighs). They'd go off to Big Sur or tour the wine country or spend a night up north in the Gualala Hotel watching old men play checkers and young men get into fights. He had lots of friends, most of whom he didn't like for more than an hour at a time. After three years of college, Eugene was settled and comfortable, having a good time of it. He had a great record collection and a favorite chair. People who loved him, a girl who worshipped him. He had it made.

But something started to nag at him. Tugging at his shirtsleeves every time he woke up in the morning to look around at his bright, sunny life. Something was starting to gnaw at him. Dig inside him. Sting and scratch and burn.

Boredom.

Eugene wanted something to happen.

Something did.

Sgt. Pepper came out.

And Mort had a heart attack.

Eugene flew down to L.A. and visited his father at the hospital. It turned out to be not much of a heart attack but it was still a heart attack. Mort was not in the best of spirits when Eugene walked in.

"Hey. What are you doing down here?"

"Flunked outta school so I thought I might as well drop in and say hello."

"How do you like this shit? A little pain in the chest and I'm rushed to the hospital."

"You know doctors."

"Yeah."

"Hey," said Eugene. "Casey says hello. He wants to know when you're comin' up so he can whip your ass on the tennis court."

"That bastard. How's he doing?"

"Pretty good."

"How's Belinda?"

"Emily."

"Emily. How is she?"

"Pretty good."

Eugene watched uncomfortably as his father was seized by a coughing spell and a sudden cramp. Eugene wished there was something he could do. He *never* knew what to do to ease other people's pain. Usually he never really cared.

"What shit," Mort said.

"Yeah."

Mort was released from the hospital and was given strict orders to cut out liquor and smokes and cut down on women. He was told to lose thirty-five pounds.

Mort started drinking very heavily. He had stopped smoking years ago but he started up again. He began to go after every woman he saw. He put on fifteen pounds.

Up in Berkeley, Eugene got a phone call. It was from Marcia, one of his father's women. Marcia was worried that Mort was killing himself. She didn't know why. Or what to do. "Come down," she told Eugene. "You're the only one he'll listen to."

Eugene came down. He wondered what he had to say that was worth listening to.

"You look terrible," Eugene told his father.

"What are you doing down here again? How's Arlene?"

"Emily. Pretty good except she tends to cry a lot."

"You here for a reason, Gene, or just to see good old dad?"

"Uh . . . well . . . sort of."

"Sort of what?"

"Sort of Marcia called me to come and see you."

Eugene saw great pain in Mort's eyes, vulnerable sorrow.

"She wanted me to give you some advice."

"You're giving *me* advice now?"

"I know. I'm gettin' older."

"A mistake."

"What? Gettin' older or givin' advice?"

"Both."

They smiled at each other. That was one of Eugene's great talents. He could smile anywhere. Mort could smile around Eugene.

"So? What's your advice?"

Eugene looked at the fat, dissipated man propped up on the bed. He zeroed in on the bloodshot eyes and what he saw was a total lack of comprehension. Gone was the curiosity to see what would happen the next day, the next hour, the following minute. Gone, too, was the desire to keep *moving* from day to hour to minute. Defeated idealism, bloated sensuality, just plain fright stared back at Eugene. There was an emptiness, a ragged edge of vapid resignation. There was, worst of all, the absence of any desire for an explanation. Eugene suddenly realized, for the very first time, that he was going to die one of these days. He suddenly saw his own skin wrinkle and sag, his body stoop, his limbs gnarl. He saw himself crawling across a floor reaching futilely for life. And he shuddered.

"I guess I don't have any." Eugene had to clear his throat. "Got any for me?"

Mort said "aaaahhhhhhhh" and put his hand on the back of Eugene's neck, grabbing a clump of hair.

"I remember the last thing I wrote. You remember?"

Eugene squinted but nodded.

"Hey. What's with that look? I know what I'm talkin' about. Whaddya, think I'm gettin' senile?"

"You were always senile."

"Best thing I ever did, that script. You remember?"

"I remember."

" 'Bout a guy. No job, gambles, lives off women, does whatever the hell he wants. Christ, I can't believe I wrote that . . . what was it, three, four years ago? I had a scene, my guy's walkin' down the street. A bum comes up to him and asks him for a dime. My guy he never carries dimes. 'I know they exist,' he says, 'but I never found them of much use.' And he gives the bum a dollar. What do you think of that?"

"It's good. It's good stuff. You know I . . ."

"You know what they used to call guys like that?"

"No."

"Dandies. Ambitious, passive, amoral. No obligations, no attachments . . . no function. You just . . . you just . . ." Mort coughed and then started choking. Eugene looked nervously around the room and finally started to reach for a glass of cloudy water, but Mort waved him off. Eugene sat still while Mort wound back down to coughing and then wheezing and then just breathing hard. "They don't exist anymore."

"Who?"

"Dandies. They're obsolete. The world's gotten too complex for people to . . . to . . ." Mort smiled. ". . . to be successful at absolute selfishness."

Eugene looked down at the floor, then back at his father. He nodded, very slowly, and smiled, very faintly. "Okay, pop," he said. "I'll watch it."

"We've had good times, haven't we?" Mort asked.

Eugene nodded.

"I remember lots of good times. I always . . . cared for you."

Eugene nodded again.

"Maybe I fucked up in some things, but . . . ." Mort shrugged.

"You did okay."

"You're gonna have trouble."

Eugene looked down.

"You don't know yet, what's to come."

Eugene smiled again. "No," he said. "I don't."

"What the hell, Gene."

"Yeah, I know. I know."

"What can I say? It's rough."

"I know." Pause. "I know."

"Love has been beaten out of me and I don't know how. What can ya do?"

"Nuthin'," Eugene murmured.

"Nuthin'."

"I know." Sigh. "I know."

Eugene went back up to Berkeley. Two months later he got the phone call that Mort had had another heart attack, a massive one, and was dead. So he went back down to L.A., forbidding a funeral, but so many people objected, Eugene said what the hell, and allowed it. Relatives from all over came to see and cry. Mort's sister, Eugene's aunt, came out from New York. She used to take Eugene for weekends when he was little and he was crazy about her when he was a boy. She gave him money for ice cream cones and let him watch horror movies in the afternoon. She always kissed him and sat him in her lap. He always thought she was perfect. Now, Eugene didn't want to touch her, or even look at her. She wore a black skirt with a gray top, her bra strap showing through the material. When she spoke lovingly, he grimaced. When she asked about his girlfriends, he shrugged. When she questioned him on his future, he didn't answer. She said they'd have dinner, he said no. She spoke of her two children and Eugene thought only of his two castrated older cousins, of their rooms at home, still occupied, still stinking of childhood. When she kissed him, Eugene had to turn away.

Wealthy, senile Uncle Roger came over to tell Eugene that Morton was a shining example of that ancient truism, money can't buy happiness. Lavinia's brother had kept in touch with Mort throughout the years, had often taken Eugene to ball games and boxing matches, to the Playboy Club once when Eugene was fifteen. Uncle Roger was a lawyer and he repeated everything twice, sometimes more, and was afraid that everyone he knew would become an alcoholic.

"I saw Priscilla," he said. "Priscilla."

"Who?"

"Your old maid. Your old maid."

"Oh."

"She looks terrific. Terrific."

"I got a Christmas card from her."

"She was with that friend of hers. That friend of hers. You know, the one she lives with. You know. That friend."

"Marge."

"*Marge*, isn't it?"

"Yeah. I think so."

"That Priscilla. I'd give her anything. Anything. She brought you up."

"I know."

"That other one, though. Her friend. What was her name?"

"Marge."

"Wasn't her friend's name Marge?"

Eugene nodded.

"Her I spit on. I spit on her. I wouldn't give her a cuppa coffee."

"Why?" Eugene asked.

"What do I owe her? Nothin'. Nothin'. She's an alcoholic. An alcoholic. Pisses away her money on booze. You don't piss your money away on booze, do you?"

"No."

"What do you piss your money away on?"

"Nothing."

"You got to! You got to piss your money away on something! That's the secret. You wanna know another secret?"

"Sure."

"You gotta want everything, but care about nothing! That's the real secret!"

Eugene said he was glad he knew the secret and Uncle Roger went off cackling and happy. Eugene had always thought his uncle was a genius until he was old enough to realize Uncle Roger was a not-very-bright alcoholic.

Mort's female flock showed up, of course, all looking at each other suspiciously, all wearing perfume or jewelry or clothes that Mort had bought for them. Writers and producers and studio execs—they *all* came. They all said nice things about Mort and felt sorry for Eugene.

And Morton Toddman's son, Eugene, quietly observing, eyes slipping out rays of discomfort, disgust, and disinterest into the unknowing throng, tried very hard to feel sad. But he didn't. Couldn't. He was sorry his father was no longer around, he had *liked* him. But the man had wanted out. And that was his privilege. Eugene had seen the agony in Mort's eyes, and Mort had made his escape from it. Mort was dead, and in the few days Eugene had had to adjust to that fact, he came to the realization that death was a viable alternative to life, a very real option, in fact, a very tangible portion of existence. An incessant reminder of the need to push life to its limits in order to give it any kind of meaning. And, at the same time, death was a constant lure, a promise of permanent relief. An eternal vacuum, preferable to many, over daily risk. That was Mort's choice and Eugene respected it. But it wasn't his choice, not Eugene's. He was opting for something else. Reaching and struggling for something different. He didn't know what but, as he saw it, life was definitely a far more interesting unknown than death.

For the rest of his L.A. stay, Eugene kept away from all the people he'd grown up with. He spoke to several lawyers, settled his affairs, and then went back up to Berkeley. A month before he was to receive his diploma, Eugene decided he'd had it and dropped out of school. It bored him. The little piece of paper signaling he'd collected four years of knowledge was no longer important to him so he didn't want to bother with it. Besides, he was rich. So he bought a ticket for New York.

"Come with me," he told Casey.

"I can't."

"Why not?"

"I can't afford it."

"I can. Come on."

"No. I'd like to."

"Well, let's go."

"I can't."

So they hugged and Eugene packed his bags and said goodbye and took off.

A change. An adventure.

More fun.

9.

The thrill was still there as was the electric vitality, and Eugene wanted his new environment to slap him, pound him, and drag him through its heart. So his first day in New York City, he walked from Ninety-third Street on the Upper West Side to Houston Street on the Lower East Side. He saw a man get hit by a car; one stabbing; several drunks lying unaided on the sidewalk; two small children playing with pieces of broken glass; and a horn-rimmed honky being chased down the street by two enormous negroes and one very mean-looking Puerto Rican. Eugene took it all in, breathed deeply of the foul, foul air, and smiled. Home.

New York:

Deciding to live for real—that is, as if there weren't lots of money tucked away in the bank—Eugene spent several weeks looking for inexpensive apartments. Poring over the *Voice* and the *Times*, running around the city visiting basements, five-floor walkups, greasy supers, rats, floorless living rooms, and wall-less bedrooms. Several months were spent *living* in a studio with no shower, no light, no air, and a large

roach that Eugene named Norman. Norman was killed when
the kitchen sink fell off the wall and crushed him. Eugene
wasted no time in moving to another chamber of the heart.
Out came the tucked-away loot and in came a two-bedroom
duplex on West Tenth. Large windows with southern exposure that let in the sun, a fireplace, brick walls, wood all
over, and a slightly deaf landlady who made it plain that
Eugene could come over and discuss rent control anytime.

He saw *The Graduate* and *Bonnie and Clyde*.

He decided he should work.

He got a job.

Working in a television-commercial production company. It
seemed as interesting as anything else. Learning production, dealing with creative people, traveling, loose hours.
He took long lunches and charged cabs to the office and
eventually produced one commercial that used a dancing
can of soup. Eugene quit in six months.

The next job, an opposite extreme, was one handed out as a
legal assistant. To a very generous overweight Jew who
chomped on cigars and handed out summonses and collection notices. Good money, long, relaxing days in court,
respectful employees, quiet evenings doing research in wood-
paneled rooms. Eugene left in five months.

Martin Luther King and then Bobby Kennedy were cut down.
College students had finally progressed from marching to
rioting, and for their efforts were either jailed or tear-
gassed. Eugene always rooted for them and had slight pangs
of longing to join in when he would read descriptions of the
action in the newspapers the next day. A lot of flabby legs
were striding around in mini-skirts. People would laugh
anytime someone tapped them on the shoulder, looked confused, and said "Sock it to *me?*" There were hard hats.
And there was Woodstock. The end of the draft, which
didn't affect Eugene either way since he'd already bought
his way out. Once out of school, Eugene's concept of time
blurred, and the next few years seemed to slip together.
Vonnegut seeped into people's consciousness, and R. D.

Laing. Archie Bunker started using bad words on TV. The Beatles were no more. Eugene cried when Ali lost to Frazier.

A job with a local magazine. One with a film company. A salesman. A copywriter. They all loved him, they had plans for him, they treated him well. Eugene kept leaving.

Somewhere, in the very early seventies, the volatile sixties ended, and Eugene felt, for the first time, that he was not so important a factor in whatever might happen in the future. Ads were no longer geared for him, clothing took on a new look that he was not one hundred percent comfortable with. For the first time ever, *Rolling Stone* was giving rave reviews to groups he'd never heard of. It was, at long last, the era of Richard Nixon. Eugene stopped taking an active interest in politics, refused to concern himself with who was running what. He had stopped caring about changing society, merely wanted to exist untroubled by it. Mays was now a .280 hitter.

Before nine in the morning and after five at night, New York whirled around Eugene. Horns honked their street music while he earned his paycheck, friends breakfasted at eleven without him. The city beckoned to Eugene over the rhythm of electric office typewriters. With an unconcerned shrug, he finally left the working world behind him, started spending his money, and entered the center of the cyclone.

Eugene lingered at all-night newspaper stands, watching steam geysers rise from mysterious holes in the pavement. He had conversations with crazy people in diners, frequented pizza stands and delis and pick-up bars, and grabbed lots and lots of excitement and lots and lots of hassles. Eugene worked out at the Sixty-third Street Y and bought food at Zabar's and window-shopped at Macy's at Christmas. He partied at rent-controlled brownstones and brazenly visited the skyscrapers that cage the endless stream of offices housing television companies, advertising agencies, newspaper bureaus. Eugene watched the media create as well as report the shape of the world and he watched New York create and control the media. He saw New York control practically everything it came in contact with. With its weather, its traffic, its dogshit. Its air conditioners that blasted during the winters and stood silent during heat waves. Its prices, its filth. Its intelligence and culture and its crippling ignorance. Eugene saw a New York that was all things to all people— flashing, popping, whirring by; embracing, enveloping, suffocating, life-giving; biting and clawing and loving. He saw it as everything that everywhere else is, only more so and better and stronger. New York as fun and excitement and everything that glitters, be it golden or tin. With everything to do. And Eugene did it. Which is what worried him.

For an old enemy struck.

Slowly, but surely . . . and unmistakably, boredom began to nibble its way back into Eugene's existence.

He fought it. He stayed out later, he drank harder. More drugs and more women. He stopped seeing old friends and made new friends. Then dropped his new friends and made newer friends. He moved from intellectual circles to rowdy scenes, sometimes dragging one life over to another, trying desperately to liven both.

Nothing worked.

He didn't understand it.

He went after many women with a supine ferocity. He had always fallen back on women to alleviate boredom. Now he *had* women. Plenty of them. None lasted long, none were able to become a part of him. They all became distant images—the feel of smooth flesh, a pair of lips softly kissing a cheek, a giggle, a pair of jeans. An easy lay. A virgin. Smoky eyes and wisps of desire.

Eugene had become a devastating lover, an all-encompassing one. He took women to their physical limits, drained them emotionally. It wasn't just semen that came pouring out of our man, it was hatred and love and passion and struggle to break through an unknown and unseen barrier. Lovemaking was forceful thrashing about, tense and hardened lurching; sudden capitulation and collapse—a head on a soft arm and

closed eyes, fingers twirling locks of hair. Eugene enjoyed
nothing as much as making love, and everything that went
with making love—the two A.M. snacks, the first-thing-in-
the-morning caresses, the sneaking away from jealous hus-
bands, the sin, the pleasure, the gentleness. Lovemaking
was the only action that Eugene found came totally naturally. It was all he had learned to offer when wanting to truly
reveal his self. And people drifted toward Eugene's self,
particularly women. Perhaps they sensed, in him, great love.
Perhaps indifference. Perhaps both—an overpowering combination. He would glide along in a relationship, never promising, never committing, never demanding. Yet tears were
shed, pain was invariably inflicted. More than anything else,
Eugene observed, his actions were followed by pain. He
came away from his dealings with people with images of
fear and confusion, dread and incomprehensible pain. Eugene
didn't understand the way people punished themselves, for
he had been, all his life, only desirous and guilt-free. He
had never feared the consequences of his actions, never
thought about any consequences. But slowly, people
demanded, and slowly, he refused to respond. And slowly,
he began to be afraid. Not a paralyzing dread, but he began
to fear that people would eventually begin punishing *him*.
And they did, of course.

It was his damned eyes.

They were curious. They *wanted*.

They got more than they bargained for.

Suzanne picked him up at a party. He was encircled by a
bunch of forty-year-old men, all divorced, all recently
transplanted from New Jersey, all with sexy twenty-three-
year-olds. Eugene was holding court, dazzling the models,
charming the executives. He told them funny stories, he
hinted at sexual conquests, he name-dropped. He'd read
every book they named, knew who directed every film they
had just seen. When he went for a refill of chili, Suzanne
was right there with the large spoon.

"Hi," she said.

Eugene smiled.

"You know Betsy Miller, I think."

Eugene smiled again. But this time added a shake of his head.

"You do."

"Do you know where the pickles disappeared to?"

"You're Gene Toddman."

"And the beer is gone. Why is there no beer? Where's the refrigerator?"

"Betsy said you were an incredible fuck."

They were back at his place in less than half an hour. They were through less than a half hour after that.

"That was great," said Eugene.

"That was incredible."

"You have good legs. Good legs."

"The way you licked my toes, my God!"

"That was great."

"That was incredible."

"Thanks," said Eugene and turned on the last half of the Knicks game.

"Geez," said Suzanne. "That's kinda rude. Donja think?"

He shrugged, kind of hoping it looked to be apologetic.

"Geez," she said again. "You want me to leave?"

Eugene swore as Reed missed a free-throw.

"Geez." She started to get dressed. "Geez-uz!"

"Don't take this the wrong way," he said, "but what was your name again?"

"Suzanne."

"Suzanne. Do you have to keep saying 'geez'?"

"Gaaaawwwwd!"

"Much better."

"You know, you weren't really so fantastic. For a guy with your reputation and all. You weren't so fantastic."

"I thought I was incredible?"

"I once fucked Warren Beatty. *He* was incredible."

"I bet."

"You want incredible, fuck Warren Beatty."

The Knicks were up by eighteen points and were substituting freely. Eugene turned toward the sexy blonde who was just getting her shoes on.

"Life!" said Suzanne. "Geeee-eeeez!"

"Life," said Eugene, "is like a basketball game. If you play too hard, all you get is a technical foul."

"Geeeezzzz!"

Leslie was a recent Sarah Lawrence graduate. She wore clothes that were just a bit too expensive for her age. Her ass was too big and she talked a lot in bed.

"I slipped out," said Eugene. "Put me back in."

"I don't think you like people."

"What?"

"I was watching you in the restaurant tonight. The way you were observing the patrons. So detached. So cool and re-moved."

"I was just about to come just now."

"You're like my husband."

"You're married?"

"Separated. You're just like Frank. Disconnected. Dispassionate. He wouldn't give."

"I give."

"Oh, you give. But only if you get."

"Oh."

"Of course, can you really give until you're complete? Hmmmm. That's interesting. Can you be complete until you take and take and take? That *is* interesting, isn't it? If you take, it might be because you want to give. So does that mean you like people or not?"

Eugene shrugged.

"You don't like people."

Now Eugene sighed.

"Admit it."

"What?"

"You don't like people."

"What's to like?"

"You see?"

"I see."

"Are you still hard?"

"What?"

"I'm stimulated."

"Stimulated?"

"Very. Are you still hard?"

"No," said Eugene. "No. I'm not."

"What a life you lead. What a life."

"Life is like a dick," Eugene said, looking down. "When it's soft you can't beat it. When it's hard you get fucked."

"I'm going home," said Leslie.

Nancy was into S-M. She wanted Eugene to spank her.

"What do you mean, spank you?"

She told him, so he spanked her.

"Would you spank me harder?"

"Spank you harder?"

"With a hairbrush."

"I thought we were going to have sex."

"I know. It's the only way I can have an orgasm. I'm sorry. I thought I could tell you. You seemed so . . . I don't know . . . I thought you'd do it."

Eugene got a hairbrush.

"I don't tell many people. But you understand, don't you?"

Eugene started to laugh. "Oh sure. I understand."

"Are you angry?"

"No."

"Tell me you're angry."

"What?"

"You gotta tell me you're angry."

"I'm angry."

"Tell me you're gonna punish me."

Eugene rubbed his eyes. "I'm gonna punish you."

"Am I your slave?"

Eugene closed his eyes.

"Am I your slave am I your slave?"

"You're my slave you're my slave."

"I came," said Nancy.

"Great," said Eugene.

"Life is weird, isn't it?"

"Life is like a whipping. All that counts," and Eugene put his hand on the back of his neck and sighed before finishing, "is that the beatings stop."

"Not with me," said Nancy.

"What do you want for dinner, darling?" asked Jane.

"Don't call me darling, okay?"

She kissed Eugene on the cheek and ran her hand through his hair.

"Don't mess up my hair, alright?"

She kissed him again and her hand rubbed up and down his back.

"What do you want for dinner tonight?"

"I don't know."

"Lamb chops?"

"No."

"A chef salad?"

Eugene stared at the ceiling.

"Jane?"

"What, sweetheart?"

"Jane. It's seven o'clock in the morning. How the fuck am I supposed to know what I want for dinner at seven o'clock in the morning?"

"You're right, my love. I'm sorry. It's my fault."

"S'okay."

"Do you think you'll want rice or potatoes?"

Eugene shook his head and shrugged.

"Should I get sugar cones?"

He didn't want to answer but he had to. "What?"

"It'll be fun. We'll make our own ice-cream cones."

"Life is like an ice-cream cone."

"How so, my pet?"

"Once you get past the soft stuff, all that's left is the crunch."

Sharon was a terrifically nice girl. She was a delicate and beautiful girl who thought she was awkward and ugly.

"Do you think I'm pretty, Gene?"

"You're lovely."

"I like my hair."

Eugene nodded, showing that he, too, liked her hair.

"I don't like the rest of me."

Eugene refused to look at her as Sharon played with the hair on his chest.

"You'll take care of me, won't you?" she asked.

Eugene got out of bed. He paced around the room. He exhaled and looked at her and shook his head.

"I don't know why I make life so difficult."

"Neither do I," said Eugene. "Neither do I."

Eugene fucked Denise, pushed hard inside her while he finished coming. He was breathing hard, gently slid himself out, grimacing. Denise told him how good he felt. Denise tried to touch him. Eugene stood up and went into the living room. After fifteen minutes, Denise followed. Eugene stared at her until she went back into the bedroom and put her clothes on.

"Did I do something?" she asked.

He didn't speak.

"You want me to leave?"

She waited in the doorway for him to answer. When he didn't, she began to fidget. When he still didn't answer, she opened the door. She left. Eugene looked out the window. She came back. Eugene didn't turn from the view of his garden. She left again.

Women cajoled Eugene, caressed and took care of him. Hated him and tried to hurt him; pleaded with him to love them, to teach them, to learn from them. They bent their flexible wills to his strong one; tried to laugh along with his laughing view of the world. He pushed them to their every limit, stuck his cock in their every orifice, bought them gifts, talked sweetly, discarded—rather, recycled—them. He burned them with his eyes, peering deep into their souls, forcing them to look into *his* until they would turn away in confusion or incompetence—inability to cope with a passionate void.

People, yes, women especially, sacrificed things to Eugene. Everything from pride and self-respect down to as minute a detail as where to have dinner or what movie to see. But this sacrifice was a front, a fraud, a tantalizing lure. For they kept the only thing that Eugene *would* sacrifice—the desire to possess. So women became part of a seductive battle, a force to conquer and to be wary of. Relationships were distorted into wars of possession, ties to be avoided at the cost of loss of self. Passion was allowed to fester and burn, but never be turned loose, never to reign unchecked.

It was weird.

He liked people but he had to stay away from them.

He found fleeting moments of ecstasy, but it wasn't enough.

He wasn't unhappy. But he was floundering.

He was drowning.

Eugene didn't understand it, this boredom. But it began to get on his nerves.

10.

A letter from Eugene Toddman to Casey Gruber:

May 16, 1972

Dear Banananose,

Uh oh. Something's happening. Or something happened. I'm not sure which.

I'm feelin' restless. I's a feelin' down an' blue, mah body's feelin' low. I did the unforgivable last night: some hot little piece of falafel wanted to come home with me and see my etchings and I said no. N-O, NO! Why did I do this foolish impetuous thing? I didn't feel like fucking her. She was cute and bubbly and impressionable (she said she luh-*uh*ved Bob Dylan), but I just didn't have the heart to ram the old magic avenger into her Hostess Twinkie.

Here's my reasoning:

We would have gone back to my apartment. She would have had a drink (she would have had several to make sure she got drunk or could fake being drunk). We would have had this ridiculous conversation—me being my usual suave, dapper, debonair self (nibbling caviar while folding my socks) and she being her cute, bubbly, impressionable, Desolation Row self—and the conversation would have been all about the theater, a new bestseller, the rising price of apartments, our choice for President (in 1996 she'll still be for McCarthy), the moral question of marijuana, life in her hometown (either someplace in Ohio or Queens, take your pick), or we might have even sat around and gotten depressed about the anniversary of Kent State. Perhaps I'm psychic. I seem to know exactly what people will say, these days, before they say it. I know what *I* will say *weeks* before I say it.

More: I would have had to be nice to her when I didn't want to. I would have had to talk when all I wanted to do—and this is an honest, sincere evaluation of my deepest psychological and physiological desires—was have her lick my entire body while I made a major deposit in the ol' sperm bank.

But I didn't.

Why? Read that "Why!"

Why? Beats me, honcho.

Maybe because the years just seem to disappear. Although to tell you the truth, I don't know what that has to do with anything. Don't panic, however. No need to send me any rolled-up trousers. Just don't dare me to eat a peach, okay?

Listen: I've developed this annoying little habit of boiling things down. I read and go to Broadway shows and see all the films that are out. All these brilliant writers inform me that either life is fucked or life is great—this is what everything seems to boil down to. Well I don't *want* to know that life is fucked or life is great—I want to know what to *do* in the meantime. Everywhere I turn, all I see and hear are words. Meaningless symbols of long-lost truths; once normal and now nonexistent desire . . .

Uh oh again. Whoops.

I just reread this and realize that I am losing my sense of humor. I will now pause to tell you a joke.

Bad news. I can't think of any jokes. You know all the Polack ones. And I doubt you'd get much of a chortle if I tossed out an old Elephant punch-line. Maybe I should just enclose a copy of *Cracked*. Or a Mad Zeppelin. Or a tape of Don Rickles insulting Ed MacMahon.

I guess you're not laughing, huh? Are you chuckling at least? As long as you're not throwing up, I'll be satisfied. Hoo ha!

So much for humor.

I am working again. With a publishing company. Thanks to skill, talent, taste and a tennis partner of mine who is vice-president of the company, I am an associate editor, and I am going to try to last at this one. Haven't worked for two years—figured I should make the attempt again. My social circle was beginning to wonder how I could keep downing Stingers at two A.M. on a Tuesday. Dat ol' Puritan Ethic is making one last attempt to clutch at my scrotum, this time it's with a "glamour" job. I know I should get excited about it. I know, I know. I should. But I can't. The other day at an editorial meeting (we have them twice a week over diet sodas and roast beef sandwiches), it was announced that my venerable company had a chance to acquire a beautiful collection of Conrad's complete works. I had barely vocalized my approval before another, more important editor asked the following question: "Who gives a fuck about Conrad?!" That ended that, as everyone realized the answer was no one. I'm probably gonna quit soon because . . . because . . . well . . . even if *I* don't give a fuck about Conrad, it seems to me that *they* should.

BAH!

Meanwhile, my money refuses to disappear (a blessing, that was not a rich boy's cynical complaint), but still I thought perhaps a job would provide something. Even if it was fresh wool.

Uh huh. Sure.

I forgot what it's like. Here's my day:

I wake up at 7:45 to the horrible blast of my alarm clock. I then 1) if there's a woman beside me, try to sample her morning glories; 2) if no woman beside me, whack off; 3) if no woman beside me and I'm feeling very tired, I turn off the alarm and fall asleep again till 8:15. Next, I force myself out of bed, first turning on the FM and letting it blare. Stumbling to the bathroom, I detour to the kitchen, turning the light on under the coffee after I stub my toe on the kitchen table. Urinate. Shower. At 8:30, pop out of the shower refreshed, rosy-cheeked, and dewy-eyed; get dressed, dry my curly locks, sip the reheated coffee. Finally—OUT OF THE APARTMENT AND INTO REALITY. Yay! I walk two and a half blocks to the subway (no snob, I)—along the way passing little old Jewish men wearing those very snappy yarmulkas; many homosexuals—oftentime in chic leather suits, Lillian; negroes wearing green platform sneakers; old people sighing and moaning; tough New Yorkers running and bumping and perspiring their way through the tired, the huddled and the poor. Now move with me onto the subway itself! Yeah! This is livin'. Taking a seat with the risk of being slammed on the head by an irate fat woman's umbrella. Then a jostling look at the *Times* sports section (Willie is fading sadly into a .250 hitter out there in San Francisco—probably the symbol of the decline of Western Civilization).

From the subway to the office.

I talk with a few fellow workers (already a comely brunette knows enough to bring me black coffee in a mug), tell a joke or two, insult a few people, try to wake up (Feiffer would love me, no?). I then read a manuscript, write up a contract, listen to some total asshole try to explain to me what'll play in Peoria, buddy-boy—sales-wise, that is. Sometimes people come into my office and ask my advice. I give it unhesitatingly. Soon it's time for a break. Small talk as I stroll around the office. Touch the back of a secretary's neck, hold on to a slim available elbow. (There are three women in the office who want to sleep with me—I don't want to sleep with them. There are two women in the office I want to sleep with—they don't want to sleep with me.) I light cigarettes—other people's, not mine—and take crowds out for drinks. Lunch with a client, lunch with a nubile secretary, lunch by myself at a museum. The afternoon is muddied with alcohol but it is much the same as morning—reading, writing letters, talking on the telephone, gossiping, strolling. Gonna change my name to Jack Lemmon.

At five o'clock I either shove my way into the subway (first buying the final edition of the *Post*—love that Mary Worth) or say fuck it and take a cab. Pass more weirdos, more perverts, more religious fanatics, more poor people with lots of children, and a handsome number of businessmen who are cheating on their wives. Home. Step into my Village pad, sip some cold white wine (Sancerre, my man, or a simple Muscadet). A few calls around town, a crowd materializes (two is rapidly becoming a crowd to my warped mind). Dinner. A) A movie; B) A play; C) Jazz; D) TV; E) A party—pick one of the above. Or if Mays is in town, Shea Stadium.

I come home (or I *am* home and *stay* home). Go to the bathroom. Have a cold drink, make my morning coffee. Bed. 7:45 in the morning again.

Repeat.

On weekends, substitute shopping, sleeping, walking, or playing football/softball/tennis for work. I smoke a few cigars (still hooked on the small Dutch jobs), read on my own (though getting rarer). Occasionally bullshit myself and do a bit of writing (bitter, cynical, wonderfully hard satiric looks at life and society—DAWK!).

I'm starting to sit home sometimes and do nothing but stare off into space. I guess it beats hanging around people who get excited when they know The Final Jeopardy Answer.

Well . . . that's pretty much it, Pizza-face. C'est moi. Est-ce que c'est ainsi pour tout le monde?

> Your pals,
>
> Fester Bestertester and Karbunkle

P.S. Two nights ago, I went out with a girl who, as our enchanted evening ended, gave me a kiss and an extra toaster oven. A toaster oven! How is it that the All-Powerful Creator allows a girl to exist who has an *extra* toaster oven? Answer *that* one and we'll have the secret of the Universe.

P.P.S. I don't even like *dancing* anymore.

P.P.P.S. I think if, ten years ago I met me today, I'd think I was a total asshole. I'm not sure, though, which is *something*.

11.

The light streamed in and Eugene awoke on the first day of his twenty-sixth year to find out that the Giants had traded Willie Mays. Mays was forty-two years old and was neither the fielder nor the hitter he once was. Eugene had even seen his idol, on a Saturday Game of the Week, stumble and fall while pursuing a fly ball, turning a routine out into a double. But still! Stoneham just *traded* him. True, Mays was returning to New York, but not gloriously. Sadly. Hanging on. The photograph on the front page of the *News* made him look just like any dumb nigger. Made him look old. Eugene drank his coffee and decided not to go into work. He called this girl he had met at a party, Marilyn, and asked her to go out with him that night. She said she had plans. He said okay. She said she'd get out of them. He hung up. He tried to remember what she looked like.

There had been thirty, forty people still left at this party when he met Marilyn a couple of weeks earlier. A lot of publishing people, some writers, actors, agents. Two dentists—cousins of the girl throwing the bash. Marilyn was with a writer, a guy who lived up in Maine and came into the city every few months to peddle a new book and make a few thousand dollars. He had peddled enough books to afford an embroidered jean suit which Marilyn hung onto.

Eugene stood around with a glass of Jack Daniels, taking a hit off a sporadically passed-around joint. Somehow he started talking to the writer's girlfriend. She was wearing too much perfume and a dress with a plunging neckline. Blue eye shadow, a couple of shades too dark, dominated her face. Marilyn was an actress, she said, although she made her money working for an advertising agency, freelancing for their art department. She was from New Jersey originally, now living on Manhattan's Upper East Side.

As Eugene drank more Jack Daniels, Marilyn stopped hanging all over Jean Suit and kept touching Eugene's arm and smiling at him. People kept coming over to them, asking Eugene what he thought about this or that, expecting him to say something witty, seeking his approval on the food or a book or a film or a woman. When the party was over, Eugene took Marilyn's phone number, asking for it offhandedly, said he'd call her. And he called. On his birthday. And when he hung up he figured that she was as interesting, as placid, as nonirritating as anyone else he'd met lately.

A few people called to wish him a happy birthday. Casey called and told Eugene he'd gotten his first decent architectural assignment. It was helping to design a restaurant, hopefully a chain of restaurants, that would serve nothing but different varieties of waffles. Casey was very excited and Eugene congratulated him. They horsed around a bit on the phone. Eugene promised a long letter and a trip to L.A. Then put down the receiver and kept his finger on the button before slowly walking away from the phone.

Eugene walked around the apartment touching things, letting his hand dawdle over tabletops, dragging his fingers around ashtrays. He opened a window, inhaled deeply, drawing in the fragrances of the Village—fresh-made bread, a touch of left-over garbage, the odor of spilled gasoline.

There was the distinct drone of Con Ed drilling underlying the day.

Evening came.

Eugene put on a three-piece suit that fit him perfectly, went uptown by cab to pick up Marilyn. As he watched her put the finishing touches on her hair and makeup and then usher the cat in from the hallway, he looked her over very carefully. The girl put herself together. She was a craftsmanlike work capable of emitting sexy vibrations and a pouty look that promised a good blow job. She was twenty-six years old, would probably look terrific for another six or seven years and then look terrible. She had long, dark, thick hair that touched her arms and sometimes flung itself around her neck. She was tall, wore low platform shoes, and, no question about it, had a Jewish body—broad hips, great tits, and thighs that were sexy, leaning toward chunky. There was something about her body that broadcast about her parents in Jersey who gave her money and credit cards; something that suggested two marriage proposals—one from a lawyer, one from a doctor (perhaps a pharmacist)—and there was something emanating from her looks (probably from the long, sharp, silver fingernails) that screamed, "This girl is sexy enough, nice enough, intelligent enough, selfish and sophisticated enough to pull off a lifetime of getting what she wants and getting it easily." Eugene wondered what she wanted. Which is why he was out with her. She would be a sagging, fat-assed, flapping mess by thirty-five, no doubt, but by then it wouldn't matter because she *did* put herself together at twenty-six.

They went out past the Puerto Rican doorman, into the swank, stewardess-infested seventies, and down into the pimp-ridden forties to see *CRASH!*, the new hit musical about the 1930s depression. There was a six-foot-six black who carried the show; he sang a song called "Freedom" in which he explained how freedom was really smellin' the flowers and hearin' the bees and feelin' the sunshine on yo' face. He also danced a dance where he jumped over garbage cans and swirled old, drunken bums around the stage. The dance showed the audience that life, even for a starving nigger, could have dignity, no matter how perverse.

Eugene and Marilyn went to Sardi's after the show, where seven people came over to their table. One of the tablehoppers was a playwright, who asked Eugene if he'd read the new Tom Wolfe piece. Eugene said that he had, then finished eating his soft-shell crab. The other twenty-second visitors raved or knocked whoever was up for raving or knocking. After a Boccone Dolce dessert, they cabbed back to Marilyn's apartment. She apologized for the mess while she put on the new Stevie Wonder album, the volume turned down low so as not to disturb the neighbors. She danced a few quick dance steps, shaking her hips a bit, making her shoulders and neck slither back and forth. She sat down next to Eugene, her hand on his thigh, one of her sharp fingernails running along a thread on his pants. She told him what a wonderful time she had, how much she loved New York theater and Sardi's, the whole ambience of the place. She mentioned an ex-boyfriend, her hang-ups in their relationship, his sickness and unwillingness to relate on a personal level. She talked about her trip to Europe a few summers before where she saw Rod Stewart before he *was* Rod Stewart. She pointed out her paintings, therapeutic (she said) extensions of her need to be loved. She said she was drunk: The Cue.

Eugene put his hand on the back of her head, firmly bringing her forward so he could kiss her. He slipped his tongue into her mouth while she moaned quietly and assuringly. Eugene ran his hands down her body, his fingers creeping into the back of her pants, grabbed her, started to wrap his legs around her. As his head slipped onto her chest, Marilyn suddenly went limp, participating no longer, neither resisting nor encouraging. It took Eugene a few moments to realize that he was pawing at a motionless object, but when he did grasp the situation, he froze. She clung to him, whimpering contentedly. Eugene glared at her, a slow feeling of frustration starting to well up inside. She moved again, gently, placing her lips against his ear, oblivious to his silent tension. Marilyn quietly whispered that she didn't know if she was ready for a *bed* trip.

"What?"

"I just don't know if I'm ready."

Eugene swallowed. There was a lump in his throat. He turned his head a few degrees away from her, picking out a strand of ill-tasting hair from his mouth.

"For a bed trip."

"Yeah," she said. "For the involvement. *You* know."

Something new, a strange sensation began to pound within Eugene.

"Uh huh."

"I just, you know, wanna *know* you. Before anything happens. You know."

Eugene's eyes blinked twice. He looked up, looked back down, twisted his neck a bit. His mouth twitched downward on the left side. A strange, strong, vibrating energy, a pulsating light that zoomed out of his eyes, careening around the room.

"So what are you thinking?"

"What?"

"What are you thinking?"

"Are you lying on my sock?"

"What?"

It swelled, bloating the entity known as Eugene Toddman. He lifted her body away from the fold of his arm. His eyes hardened, grew cold. He got his socks, pulled on his pants, put on his coat, patted the girl's shoulder as he nodded at her and walked out the front door. He numbly made it down three flights to ground level. Outside, this powerful new awareness stung as if a cold, winter wind, whipping him back and forth, cutting and slashing at his insides.

It finally happened.

He was angry.

Angry that there was a girl who had big tits who kept them to herself. Angry that there were people who sold blueberry waffles who could control other people's lives, and angry that the only options he could find still around were untruths or unfulfillment. Angry that everywhere he looked he saw nothing but people existing for the sole purpose of taking the pleasure out of life. Livid because the world was out of control and the simple thing of it was that people didn't know what the fuck they were doing. Eugene included.

Anger.

It's a dangerous sensation, for it reinterprets the past. The good becomes stagnant, the sweet and the tender turn bitter and cruel. As Eugene's anger spread, the images that were his life floated by, and suddenly they were harrowing, ugly, meaningless shadows. Eugene squinted at his existence and saw a connect-the-dots puzzle with no looming figurehead to pencil in his reality. He didn't know why, he didn't even understand, yet, what it was he was feeling. Only that it was incomprehensible, unsatisfying, all-encompassing. Only that he wanted to feel something else. But he didn't know what. Or how. He was stumped.

And so, in the now-drizzling rain, Eugene walked the entire fifty-five blocks home from Marilyn's apartment, stopping off along the way only to buy a thin cigar. He smoked it while he walked, shaking his head every so often, a barely perceptible gesture.

And when he made it home, Eugene fell into a deep sleep—the emotions can be physically exhausting—until very early the next morning when his phone rang. A squeaky voice informed Eugene Toddman that his Uncle Roger had died, at long last, of old age and a dissolved liver. Eugene, as the sole heir, would receive over two hundred and fifty thousand dollars. Eugene rubbed his eyes and hung up. He felt no strong emotions upon hearing of his uncle's death. By this time death was, to Eugene, nothing more than a debt one had to pay to nature. In this case there was a break—the debt was paid and there was plenty left over for Eugene. So he went back to sleep and then within a few days Eugene sold almost everything he owned, made legal and financial arrangements for his new inheritance, and left the country. Tired of people, of pressure, tired of *life;* hoping to retreat, at least to sift through a disordered mind and see what was left. Hoping to avoid the confusion and the complexities of civilization. Hoping to escape the evil and the destruction from without and the boredom from within. To embrace the masterpieces of literature, inflame himself in the beauty of poetry; to marvel at the glories of nature, consume himself within the power of the elements, make love to country wenches. To reduce and to simplify. To rediscover, perhaps to *discover* truth and beauty. After years of disjointed images that failed to solidify or grow or thrive, to lead a perfect life.

That's what he was hoping for, all right.

Part Two

12.

"*Qui est-il?*" the baker asked his wife.

"*L'Americain,*" she said, and as she said it, turned away from her husband to smile accommodatingly at the customer. Her very lovely breasts brushed against the glass counter. "*Bonjour, monsieur.* What can I do for you?"

"Ohhhh . . . just pick out a few pastries. I'll trust your judgment."

"*Bon. D'accord.*" Her voice trailed off on an upward note in that strictly French manner, and she began to make her selections. The man behind the counter nodded at his customer as their eyes met.

"*Quel Americain?*" the baker now asked.

"The American who moved into Paulette's old house."

"*Ah oui. Ah oui.* What's his name?"

"*Je ne sais pas.*"

As his wife busied herself, the baker looked the American over. The man was dressed casually, though impeccably. He was the type who seemed formally dressed even when wearing the most informal of jeans. There was an uncaring attitude about the American—he didn't even choose

93

his own pastries, an unforgivable indifference in the eyes of the baker. There was an insolence, a lackadaisical curiosity, a provoking removedness. This man had something about him, though, the baker decided. He felt this man was worth starting a conversation with.

"How do you like living in our town?" he began.

The man nodded, an assertion that he found the living pleasant enough.

"Are you married?"

"No."

The baker laughed.

"What, a good-looking young man like you? What are you waiting for?"

"*Rien.*"

"You live alone?"

The man nodded.

"You're waiting for a girlfriend then, eh?"

The American smiled. Then shook his head. "Never wait for girlfriends," he said. "Bad habit."

"Ah," said the baker. "You should be French if you already know that."

The American kept the grin on his face. He liked the baker. "Anything else you'd like to know?"

"Sure," and the baker grinned back. "What do you do and what do you think?"

"*You're* French, yes?"

"Of course. *Bien sûr.*"

"Then *you* should know that what you think ain't got much in common with what you do."

"Here you are, *monsieur,*" the baker's wife chirped, handing over her selections. And then she leaned over the counter and whispered, "I'll see you tonight, yes?"

"No," said the American. "Not tonight. *Pas ce soir.*"

Eugene Toddman strolled out of the *patisserie* and, before heading up the street, took another look around the town of Sancerre.

It's a little French village, toward the northeast part of the Loire region, built amidst rolling hills, surrounded by thriving vineyards, populated with stone farmhouses and ancient chateaux. Up above the river, overlooking the winding current. A few small hotels usually reserved for travelers leisurely passing through on their way elsewhere. One department store, even a red-light district. But a small town. Most everyone knows most everyone else. The cafés at night brim over with wine-induced familiarities and heated struggles over pinball. Newspapers are deliverable on a handful of bicycles and one jeep. Several families compose the wealthy class, the rest are workers or small farmowners. The people are friendly; the world is kept, for the most part, at bay. And, for some reason, there are usually, in Sancerre, laughing children in the streets.

Eugene, the doughy odors of the bakery following him, wandered over to the schoolyard to talk with the children in quiet, earnest tones. He had read somewhere that Salinger used to spend his days talking with children in schoolyards. Secretly he hoped that their purity could rub off a little. So Eugene would often wrestle with the smaller ones or join in a game of soccer. They thought him nice and funny, he enjoyed their willingness to indulge in pure frivolity. And Eugene's French was short of superb; it was an extra treat to throw slang back and forth with his young chums. They talked about American football and about teachers and vegetables and girls.

"Hey, Gene," one tough little seven-year-old interrupted.

"Yah?" This was an odd habit Eugene had developed. He raised his voice at the end of this one word. Being in a foreign-speaking country, he developed a syllable that he used to mean almost anything he wanted.

"What do you *eat* in America?"

"Yah?"

"Do you eat hamburgers?"

"We connoisseurs do."

"You eat hot dogs?"

"Who doesn't?"

"Spinach?"

"Bleaaahhhh."

"My mother makes me eat spinach."

"I know. It's a tough world we live in."

"Gene," said a ten-year-old. "Where's Texas?"

"It's all the area between New York and California."

"Are there cowboys?"

"Oh yeah."

He picked up the seven-year-old, lifting him onto his shoulders.

"Were you ever a cowboy, Gene?"

"Heyyyyy." He winked at them. "I'm *still* a cowboy."

Eugene put his friend down upon another little guy's shoulders just as the bell rang for class. He looked after the dispersing crowd, watched them run and skip and heard them hoot as they went indoors. Eugene looked up at the sky, shrugged, and smiled. He turned away.

It was toward the end of September and unseasonably cold, so Eugene stuck his hands inside the pockets of his long fur coat as he now trekked back through the town. Not very many people said hello to him.

Nearly four months before, when Eugene had first come to Sancerre, he moved in quietly, trying to stay as much to himself as possible. He had carried his anger and resentment across the Atlantic with him and decided that he had no wish to open himself up to more of the same—no desire to cause pain or to have it inflicted. He wanted to stay entirely away from the stuff. He rented a wooden off-white house which sat on the outskirts of town. There were fifteen acres surrounding his new home, including a small pond and a few straggling grape vines. Paint peeled off a few boards on the outside of the house as well as on the walls of a couple of rooms inside. But on the whole it was in good shape. Five bedrooms, a living room, a large kitchen, a study. Plenty of comfortable furniture—big cozy chairs, a cast-iron stove, wooden hutches. Eugene rented the house the day after he landed in France. The furniture was included and so was the total effect—one of comfort and warmth. To this Eugene added seclusion and self-containment.

But it is difficult, when living in a small French village, to maintain the distance from other people that Eugene had in mind. Word soon got out that there was a good-looking, wealthy young American who didn't know a soul. People dropped by, brought him bread and cakes and bottles of homemade wine. He was invited out often and had many a homecooked meal delivered to his doorstep. For a short while Eugene enjoyed his company. He relaxed and eased into the comfort of having regular visitors and hearing voices. Enjoyed watching the old women on their bicycles, the jaunty slant of the old men's berets. The handshake of recognition from the café owners. It was these small things that made his eyes radiate with pleasure and a sense of belonging. And he loved listening to the French philosophy. The old people seemed wise and content. They appeared to lack desire and ambition, which was Eugene's desire and ambition. He met an old goatherder in front of a castle. Eugene had thought the building was a ruin, but signs appeared proclaiming it as private property.

"This castle," Eugene asked of the goatherder, "it's private?"

"*Oui.*"

"That's amazing."

"What's amazing? *Your* house is private, *his* house is private."

"I mean," smiled Eugene, "that the owner must have a lot of money."

The little man made a "pphhh" sound with his cheeks.

"He has more money than me."

When Eugene said nothing, the goatherder asked Eugene if he were French.

"American," Eugene answered apologetically.

"French, American," the goatherder said. "What's the difference?"

And then he whistled and two dogs and two hundred goats came galloping toward him, raced into the hills, and disappeared from view in a few short minutes. On his way home, Eugene somehow felt that he'd stumbled upon something important and wondered if there were any rumors of God being in the Sancerre hills. For a week afterward, he tried to find the goatherder again but couldn't. And as more time passed he couldn't find anyone else, either, whom he wanted to talk with. And so eventually his old anger pushed itself over the top and Eugene cut himself off again.

He grew uncomfortable with the tradition of old France—

the religion, the snobbery, the nationalism, the protective families, the chauvinism. Yet he disliked the changes due to modern times—the greed, the mechanization of minds and actions, the architecture, the loss of and contempt for simple romance. It occurred to him that perhaps he was capable of living only at a distance, that the closer he moved to something the less desirable it proved to be. This made him angrier.

Nothing anyone said had even the slightest fascination for him after only a few minutes of conversation, and he no longer wanted to exert himself enough to have to slip on a mask, be it one even merely of passing interest. A farmer would come by, talk about the weather. A housewife stopped off, complained about rising prices. A priest, to sip a brandy and discuss apathy. Eugene was civil to them all, but curt and firm. He wanted no part of them. He was not interested in conversation. Talk, he'd found, rarely led to a viable working philosophy. Stimulus was what he needed, a physical and mental propulsion back into the functioning world. He needed solitude or a fulfillment worthy of breaking his solitude. He got neither.

Angrier and angrier.

Women came by. Some attractive and nice, some just attractive, some just nice. A few were neither, but they came anyway. Some that were for the taking, Eugene took. "Oh, *mon dieu*, take me!" one of them actually said. Eugene had to pass on her because he was laughing too hard. But on the whole, he took the bait if it was offered.

Trying to capture the glory of his dreams, Eugene would gently lull them into bed, captivated by their bodies and their musical accents. Falling in love with a few strands of hair or perhaps a voice, all such passions disappeared as quickly as they arose. Flaws produced displeasure. Disruption. Soon, even all civility was gone and, except for a whore now and then or a stray civilian encounter, Eugene withdrew into a hermetic existence.

That worked for a while.

He took long walks. Through the woods, into the sunsets, slowly into town to catch a movie in the old and tiny theater. He would sit upon the front porch in an ancient rocker for much of the day. Reading. Thinking. Waiting for the present to glide by. To Casey he wrote, "There is nothing so satisfying as being in the French countryside during an autumnal dusk. Environment becomes all; it captures and directs the emotions, the intellect, the senses. To sit amidst the approaching shadows and the shifting light—the first touches of the seasonal chill shivering body and soul—is to understand the cheap red wine and the cafés, the women and the style, the joy, the philosophers, the age."

Thus he spent his days, then his weeks, and then his months. And when Casey wrote back to him, "Are you happy?" Eugene replied promptly, "Well, perhaps not forever, but satisfied for now."

Eugene had been rocking peacefully for almost four months, as he returned from his village stroll. Stomping the late-September frost off his boots, starting to unbutton his coat, he saw the letter stuck under his door. It was a blue aerogram, though hand-delivered, with only Eugene's name scrawled on the front. It read:

My dear compatriot,

I have been residing with French people for six weeks and need to speak my native Americanese. I am refined, witty, intelligent, perceptive, and I recognize beauty when I see it. I also have a bottle of very excellent cognac which I might be induced to share with a worthy conversationalist.

I have heard much, and am *burning* to meet you.

I shall consider that I have now invited myself, rather than wait for a formal invitation. In the hope that we become partners in adventure and discoverers of the spirit of the age, I am

Your humble servant,
Lenny Latimer

Eugene smiled at the idiocy of the letter. The first thing he wondered was what there was about himself that was worth burning to meet. Eugene started to throw the note into the fireplace, then smoothed it out and placed it on his bookshelf. He poured a spot of cassis into a glass of white wine. Lenny Latimer, he thought. Crazy note. Crazy person. Who the hell would want to discover the spirit of the age? That was for another time. And different people. At least, a different person than himself. And why didn't the soup-brain call? The age certainly allowed for the spirit of a telephone. Or at least pop over? Or just stay the hell away? Oh well. It's probably tough on someone wanting to go through life as an eighteenth-century swashbuckler when he's stuck with a name that should belong to a comic-strip rooster. Eugene shook his head. But sipping the *kir*, he began to wonder if perhaps he were due for a change.

The change came three days later with a knocking at the door. Eugene knew, somehow, who it was waiting to be let in. And he knew that he didn't want to see him. And he knew he would. Eugene got pissed at himself and went to open the door.

"Monsieur Toddman?"

"Yah?"

"Lenny Latimer."

Eugene sized up the gangly kid in front of him. Longer than shoulder-length hair. Light brown. Hair that actually had to be described as flowing. A thin, finely combed moustache, the faint trace of a goatee, kind of reddish-brown. Over a red shirt that had, despite the cold, two buttons open at the neck, he wore a black cape. Not really wore. Modeled. It almost reached the floor and it rippled as a breeze came through from somewhere in the house. Black pants were tucked into high, dark leather boots, polished to reach a shining gloss. His face was proud, an adjective Eugene tried to shake away but couldn't. He was smiling, a firm, defiant smile, his lips parted confidently. Eugene was immediately sorry he had no sword to offer the young intruder. And then he realized that the last thing he'd want this person to get his hands on would be a sword. For he had crazy eyes. Very round and set deep into his face. They didn't glow, they didn't shine. They flashed and didn't so much overpower as cause discomfort. They darted and searched. They were crazy eyes, Eugene thought. He was looking into crazy eyes.

"I'm Lenny Latimer."

"I figured." Eugene cast his eyes toward the large room. "Come on in," he said. *"Entrez."*

The fire was a good one, the house was nice and warm. Lenny spoke quietly and confidently with a Southern accent that occasionally broadened and jarred the senses.

"You received mah note, I trust."

"Thanks for the advance warning."

"Ah'm staying with a French family fairly near here. A baker and his wife. The wife talks to me about you all the time."

"Does she know me, at least?"

"Madame Brunet."

"I saw her just the other day," Eugene said, and noticed that Lenny was smiling broadly. "Yah?" Eugene asked.

"You are to be commended, that's all. She's a worthy choice."

"Might you also be dipping into her chocolate soufflé on occasion?"

The look on his visitor's face showed Eugene that his assumption was a false one.

"I'm living with her and her *husband*," Lenny replied. "And that would be dishonorable." He faced Eugene directly, removed his cape, folded and placed it over the back of a chair. "I never do *anything* dishonorable."

"Ah," said Eugene. "In that case, would you like some tea?"

They had their tea and Lenny said his bones were warmed. While Eugene puffed on a cigar, Lenny strode about the house. He bent over, leaning in close to several pictures, his eyes focusing as if examining each brush stroke in a fine oil painting. He looked out the window once or twice, cackling. He turned to Eugene.

"Twenty-three years old," he said, "and I'm on top of

the world." And he laughed some more, this time a deep and hearty outburst.

You cracker asshole, Eugene thought, but shook his head, almost paternally. What do you need with me, what do I need with you? He scowled and then asked, "You bring the cognac?"

Lenny continued to laugh for no reason and, out of good-naturedness on Lenny's part and boredom on Eugene's, they became friends.

A few weeks after they met, they were drinking in Eugene's house. Lenny downed mugs of beer and was mildly drunk. Eugene sipped coffee and cognac from a long narrow glass and was waiting for a cute young university girl, home for a weekend, to come by.

"Ah'm a poet, you know," Lenny said.

Eugene smiled over his drink. "I'd suspected as much."

"A published poet."

Eugene raised his glass in an acknowledging toast.

"Ah'd like you to heah some. It's very frustrating not being able to speak and communicate the way Ah *need* to communicate. Sometimes Ah *burst* with words over here."

"I guess you poets do a lot of burning and bursting," Eugene said.

"We do," said Lenny. "I do, at least." He leaned way back, stretched his arms out, then stretched them upward, as high up as he could go.

"I'll read your poems," Eugene said suddenly. "Instead of hearing them. If that's allowed."

"It's allowed, but why?"

"Dunno. I usually understand things much better without the human voice interfering with my understanding."

Lenny seemed puzzled, but he agreed. They drank for a little bit, without talking. Lenny could tolerate only so much silence, however.

"Love is mah life's theme," he said. "What's yours?"

"I'm not a poet."

"We all have themes. Something we live by."

Eugene shrugged.

"A code, an orderly view. Honor. Or love. Or chivalry. Something to believe in, to follow you wherevah you go."

Eugene yawned and Lenny leaned forward, as if a vision of drunken paranoia. He said slowly, "I came here to live and to create. Why did you?"

Eugene poured some more brandy into his coffee, now lukewarm. "Why did I *what?*"

"Why *did* you come to Sancerre?"

There was a tapping at the door and Eugene moved to answer it. But before getting up, he revealed his great secret to Homer's eager disciple.

"It's my favorite white wine," he said.

They sat again, a week or so later, listening to music and playing chess. Lenny had carried with him from home an antique chess set with towering, hand-carved figures that looked as if they remembered being manipulated by the great kings of England's past. Eugene and Lenny had played six games in a row, Eugene winning them all.

After realizing that he couldn't possibly win the seventh game, Lenny leaped to his feet and jabbed at a log in the fireplace.

"Why haven't you bought this place," he asked, "instead of just renting? With your money, I'd buy this place and ten more like it around the world."

"I like to use things without owning them, I guess," was Eugene's answer. "I don't really have that much money."

"No?"

"No."

"You live like it. What will you do when it disappears?"

Eugene shrugged, flicked an ash onto a dirty plate.

"Can you live without money?"

Eugene smiled. "I can live without anything."

Lenny sprung across the room and began to fumble with a pile of papers on a table. He lifted up the papers and held them lovingly above his head. "My poems," he said. "You never told me what you thought of them."

"I'm not a critic," Eugene said.

"But you can react."

"Yes. I do that well."

"What was your reaction?"

"I hated them."

"Why?"

"Because you're so in love with words."

"You found no meaning *behind* the words?"

"There was meaning."

"Then your objection was . . ." Lenny stood over Eugene with an empty beer mug.

"Anyone who's so in love with *anything* can't possibly know how to use it well."

"Let's have another game of chess," Lenny laughed. "You're a worthy adversary, Gene."

They were out riding, at Lenny's insistence. It was a beautiful day. Sunny, cold, no wind. Eugene was comfortable on a horse, he felt at ease, he had a feel for the motion. He watched Lenny, fifty yards ahead. His cape was swung over his shoulder and it sailed behind him as he galloped. Off to the side there was a fallen tree, branches extending, spread over the base. Lenny drew his horse around, bypassed the obstacle, then stopped his horse about a hundred feet farther on. He pulled the reins, swung the horse back toward the rotting wood. He took off. Sped straight for the tree, straight on a line toward Eugene, the horse's legs practically floating over the covered ground. Eugene watched Lenny arch his body and cling to the horse as they glided over the outstretched branches, smoothly settling on the other side of the blockade. Eugene had seen the awkwardness and he had seen the fear cross Lenny's face at the moment of the jump. And now he saw the mad grin that Lenny flashed as he rode toward Eugene. The mad grin and the conquering eyes and the triumphant arm waving. Lenny pulled up alongside Eugene and they rode straight ahead, together, passing the site of the jump, Lenny glaring down at it contemptuously.

"I was afraid," said Lenny.

"I know," said Eugene. "I saw."

"Life is a series of fearful moments meant to be conquered."

"Is that right?"

"Taking that fear and breaking it, getting sucked up by and disappearing in the glory of the challenge. Man, that's living."

"Is it?"

"It is, boy. It is."

Eugene nodded, unconvinced.

"Why don't you jump it?" Lenny challenged, but Eugene just smiled and shook his head. "You won't take any risks at all, will you?"

A look of annoyance passed across Eugene's face but he cleared it away.

"Lenny," he said, "I'm a good horseman. In fact, I'm an excellent rider. Now how high is that tree off the ground?"

"About two feet."

"That's right. Maybe three."

"Maybe."

"You see, because I'm good I can practically step over that. It's not a risk."

"So . . ."

"So why don't I find something high enough so it might be dangerous?"

Lenny nodded.

"Because it'd be so high that that wouldn't be a risk either. And it wouldn't be livin'."

"What would it be?"

"Sudden death."

Eugene sat by his window looking out, as Lenny walked toward the house. He dodged about, twisting and turning his body. Leaping and laughing and jumping. As he drew closer, Eugene saw that he had a long walking stick in his hand. He was thrashing it about, zigzagging it through the air as if it were a saber. He was fighting off imaginary foes, thwarting their evil deeds, gallantly and valiantly holding his own. He looked up to see Eugene staring at him and Lenny momentarily dropped his pose, abashed at being caught at play. Then he jumped high into the air, shrieked, and jabbed his magic sword in Eugene's direction, charging the house in glorious defeat.

They were walking back from the schoolyard together. Eugene was playing with a small tear in his jeans. Lenny was trying to twist his leather hat to the proper jaunty angle.

He talked, of course, as they moved. Lenny loved to talk. Especially about truth and love and the human soul. He loved the sound of words, would throw quotes at his friend just to share the beauty of syllables rolling off his tongue. Now he was off on Baudelaire, he moved on to Oscar Wilde, made it to personal freedom, and shifted, a smooth transition, over to a subject he was a self-proclaimed expert on.

"Love is magic," Lenny declared.

"Yah," Eugene grunted.

"It's a magic guide."

"To what?"

"To what's right."

"And what's right?"

Lenny put his hand on Eugene's shoulder now, stopping him.

"A few months ago . . . while Ah was teaching poetry in Atlanta . . . Ah met this girl down there. A French girl." Lenny hesitated. He motioned Eugene to move even closer. "She was travelin'," he went on in a hushed tone, "for her vacation."

Eugene raised his eyebrows.

"This girl," said Lenny, and here he accented every syllable as if the words themselves were of the utmost urgency, "was rich and beautiful and smart . . . she was *everything*. She was perfect. It was amazing."

He looked up to see Eugene's reaction, which was simply one of expectation. Lenny continued.

"And she stayed in Atlanta for two weeks. Then left."

They walked till they came to a small pond.

"She lives here," Lenny said. "In Sancerre."

Eugene stopped and put his hand on Lenny's arm. "Do you mean that you just came over here hoping to find this girl?"

"Ah found her."

"Well, where is she? I haven't noticed the perfect woman hovering around you whenever we've been together."

"You'll meet her."

"When?"

"She wants me to come to her house. Meet her family. She lives like a princess . . . in a mansion. Unsullied.

Untouched. A picture, a statue. Almost unreal, like from out of the past.''

"Are you sure she *is* real?"

"Like a walking poem."

"Does she give good head?"

"Don't," said Lenny.

"Well," said Eugene, "Keats is dead, so I've heard."

"This girl seems to bring him back to life." Lenny's voice deepened and his words drifted out dreamily. "Women are life to me, Gene. Something to seek out, something to find truth in. Ah lose my center of reality when Ah fall in love. Ah have something to protect, something to worship."

"Dames is grief."

Lenny kicked at a tree. "Ah wish Ah'd lived . . . some other time. When there was *meaning* to love . . . and order to it." Now Lenny looked up at Eugene to see if he were sharing this sense of wonder and bewilderment. Eugene revealed nothing. "Do you think Ah'm crazy?"

"Yeah."

"Well . . . that doesn't matter."

"No."

"Are they . . . are they just *women* to you?"

Eugene scratched at his beard and looked down at the ground. "Yeah, Lenny. They're just women to me."

"Ah'm glad Ah don't think like that. Ah don't know what it would make me do. It would make me cruel."

"I'm glad you don't think like that, too, then."

They walked in silence. Then Lenny stopped walking and he asked Eugene to come with him.

"Where?"

"To meet her."

"When?"

"I'll call her."

"No."

"Why?"

"I don't mix well with princesses," Eugene said.

"You will," said Lenny. "I'll show you the magic."

Eugene didn't want to go. He found Lenny ridiculous. He had no desire to make contact again with young love. He didn't want to go and have to *tolerate* a day, which is what he knew he'd have to do. He didn't want to extend himself, or share any burdens, or even joys. He didn't relish participating in an illusion, be it magical or otherwise. He wanted to be left alone.

But, befitting a lifetime's pattern, his words were different from his thoughts. He pulled a branch from a tree and flung it way into the distance. It made a crashing sound in the silence and Eugene figured what the hell. What could happen?

"Sure," he breathed. And then shrugged. "Why not?"

"You won't regret it," Lenny said. "It'll be like stepping into a fairy tale. And she even has a beautiful little sister," he said. "Nicole. And mine is Hélène. Hélène Wickes."

"Uh huh."

"I'm a romantic, Gene."

"No, Lenny. You're an idiot."

"Nicole, *et* Helllllll-eeeeeeennnnnnn."

"Sure," said Eugene. "Why not?"

So Eugene spent the rest of that afternoon listening to Lenny spouting Donne at his most sentimental and Blake at his most simplistic. He wondered what the hopelessly chivalrous would-be poet really *thought* behind those cloudy eyes.

As the day wore on, Eugene wondered about love and what it was and whether it was real and, by six in the evening, he had dismissed his friend's notions and his life.

13.

Idiot or not, Lenny had not exaggerated in his description of his loved one and her family. They were the wealthiest and best-known people in the area, and they made themselves known through everything they owned and everything they did.

The head of the family, Monsieur Henri Wickes, was by this time fat and joyful, both as a result of his owning the largest, best, and most successful vineyard and winery in the area. He was a man to whom money no longer meant anything—except perhaps enjoyment. His father had been rich and his father's father had been rich before him. He grew up picking grapes in the fall and, in the summer, toughening himself up working on an uncle's fishing boat. He was wise and excitable and likable. Very French—meaning very unconcerned about his future, dismissive of his past, too caught up working hard and enjoying himself to worry about his present. He loved giving advice and showing off his scars and drinking Picon with Perrier. Henri was a good card player and a good husband. Good father. A good man. Flawed, of course, like all men, but his flaws were forgivably selfish ones. He knew no hardship and desired never to know one, so used his francs to buy food and drink and women. And then whatever made his family happy.

Elise Wickes, nearing forty-five, still had her considerable beauty. But despite her pageboy blonde hair, her long legs and thin hips, her small, firm breasts, her smooth neck and elegant long fingers, it was a beauty blunted by her cold eyes. Unlike her husband, Elise had been poor; a country girl who, thanks to a magnificent body, coquettish glances, a false pregnancy, and very Catholic parents, married into wealth. This was something she had been told always to do, and once she'd done it, had no idea what to do next except cling selfishly to her prize—her money. Eventually, Madame Wickes learned to make her husband and family her life. And, as she got older, as they grew up to appreciate her less and less, Elise forced herself to love them more and more. It was either that or succumb to her boredom and frustration. That was unthinkable for a woman of her background and her pride. Like many French women, Elise went through her awkward years in her early twenties. From a lively, sensual teen-ager, she turned straight into a bland housewife. Still, like many French women, Elise did not succumb to her pregnancies, her middle-of-the-night feedings, her marital problems, her own neurosis. So by the midthirties, instead of beginning a weary decline, she rebloomed. Her figure got better, firmer; her hair got softer, silkier; her smile got sexier, more knowledgeable. She became a woman. Unlike females of other nationalities who seem to go from being girls to being *old* women, Elise got better with age and, with one or two affairs, she managed quite nicely.

Probably the best thing that Henri and Elise Wickes did with their lives was to produce their two children, for they had truly created the wonders of the area.

Hélène was the first daughter, light like her mother, carefree like her father. If she had lived in Victorian times she would have been called a flirt. If, in her own time, she had carried through half of what she began, she would have been called a hooker. As it stood, she was neither. Merely a beautiful girl of twenty-two who had smiling eyes, an uncaring intellect, and a knowledge that she could make most men do most things without giving up much of herself. Hélène had grace and charm, her limbs moved lyrically, her animated face was divine to behold. She used her money well, spent casually yet splendidly. And she kept the look of money in her *eyes*, in the tilt of her head, not in her possessions.

She had traveled the world during her summer vacations and her Christmas holidays. Finally finishing at the university, Hélène had gone to the States, a longtime dream. Unexcited by the known quantity of the males around her, she detested Italian men and knew enough not to compete with Scandinavian women. She had met enough American men to know she liked them—enjoyed the respect they gave to women, languished in the adoration they gave to beautiful women. She had seen television shows of Disneyland and she had heard that New York was the most exciting place in the world. When finally in the land of opportunity, she went from coast to coast, stocked up on American jeans, smoked a lot of marijuana, flaunted her Frenchness, met Lenny, had a great time, and caused several men, the youngest eighteen and the oldest forty-seven, to fall desperately in love with her.

Hélène was smart, smart in the way of a sensual woman. Quiet and perceptive in her dealings with the opposite sex. Without saying anything, she had and kept that knowing sort of smile. And she would use it to great effect on those who understood and those who would fall for it. Hélène had not an ounce of romance within her. She had no imagination. Nor did she need either.

There was no hope for a young man in love with Hélène. Her looks and her smile overpowered youth and her ways gobbled it up. Few could help but want her.

Seventeen-year-old Nicole was the "different" one in the Wickes family. She had inherited all of her father's lascivious passion for life but none of his tastes with which to fulfill her desires. Drink did not go down well, men were okay, yes, even tinglingly exciting at times, but none had, as yet, lit up her soul with the overpowering romance she so desperately needed. From her mother came a dowry of delicate scorn for those around her, yet Nicole neglected to build up the outward charm and elegance that enable the rich or beautiful to get away with contempt. She was not yet a complete woman. She did not yet desire to be one.

Her skin was very white and her limbs were long, bony. She looked like a peasant, defiant and strong, at all times longing for her freedom. Nicole had a sense of humor, which showed. She also was capable of hating fiercely, which also showed. When she would brood silently around the house she was striking, wild, melancholy, and remote.

While men flocked around Hélène, they feared Nicole. Those who braved her distance or her silent ridicule did so mainly out of a craving to shatter her reserve and her superiority. Some actually found her unattractive, others were captivated by her dark beauty. The few who managed to delve past her outer shell found endless supplies of warmth and energy. She found little to expend her glow for, however. Nothing pleased her, thrilled her, and she had a dread fear of one day waking up and realizing that she had settled for contentment.

Nicole Wickes, in her tight jeans and Parisian tank-top jersey, lived worlds apart from the people she touched. She had traveled and she'd gone to school, although quitting after her first year of university, and she'd socialized and she'd done most of what teen-agers do. But always she withdrew into literature, finding centuries in which to hide between her actions, in which to live out the worlds of Richardson and Defoe and Austen and Rousseau.

This was the family anxiously awaiting the two Americans. Awaiting Lenny, to see who would have flown four thousand miles for their eldest daughter and awaiting Eugene, curious to see, finally, the figure of notoriety he had so undesiredly become.

The Wickeses lived about three miles from Eugene's house and, though Eugene had a car, an old Citroën, he decided they should walk. So the two set out through the woods, the whole way Lenny frothing at the mouth picturing Hélène, conversing about the wonders of love and nature while Eugene accepted the wind's bite and felt constantly at his freshly trimmed beard.

As they strolled up the front of the Wickes estate, Lenny noticed that Eugene had his hand covering a yawn.

"Bored already?" he asked.

"No," Eugene said. "Merely habit."

And then they were inside.

The Wickeses were not disappointed, nor was Lenny. As for Eugene, he kept himself entertained. At first with the conversation, making sure that his French was not only accurate and accented properly, but taking care to throw around his newly learned colloquialisms. The subject matter itself, ranging back and forth between poetry and literature, hunting, the vineyards, the daughters, was merely part of the setting, like the trees or the lawn or the clouds.

Hélène, the temptress, Eugene immediately dismissed. Great-looking but empty-headed. The kind who could, if he let himself go, twist him around her little finger for as long as her sensual thrill could last. But not a second longer. Once, during the late afternoon, he had a glimmer of hope for her, when he noticed that she was as bored with the chatter as he was. But Eugene decided, immediately after, that her boredom was the result only of her being out of the center of the conversation. He watched as she slipped her fingers into Lenny's hand. Delighted, distracted, Lenny twirled them back and forth, letting the new topic lapse.

At some point during the day Lenny, winking at Eugene, asked about Nicole, only to receive an agitated reply from her father.

"*Quelle emmerdeuse!*" he spat. "She decided she would rather stay up in her room than have to act like a civilized person!"

The obvious jewel of the family, Eugene decided, and the way they said the name, *Nee*-cole, made her sound lovely. The syllables were crisp, the rhythm inviting.

"She is a spoiled bitch," continued Henri. Hélène laughed

patronizingly. *"C'est vrai!* I know it! But it's too late for me to do anything!"

As he poured himself some more wine, Elise leaned over to the guests and explained that there had been a family argument. "We are planning a huge party for Hélène's birthday. A friend of my husband's, of ours, is coming from Paris for the night. We only asked that Nicki be his escort. Especially since it is unlikely she will bring one of her own."

"She said 'No dice,' " Hélène whispered. Lenny smiled at her as if she had just demonstrated Einstein's theory of relativity, and Eugene rolled his eyes and coughed. As he turned his head, he caught a glimpse of a dark-haired girl watching him from a window. Watching *him,* not them. His gaze lingered, the girl let him size her up. She stood, modeling for him, inviting him, and there was an immediate flicker of interest in his eyes which his brain tried instantly to erase. His glance, which was always a surprisingly scrutinizing one, caught one detail which leapt out at him.

Her gray eyes.

Eyes that, even as she disappeared from the window, hung in Eugene's mind. He spotted something in the girl's eyes. Something which he knew well, always recognized, usually sympathized with. It was a haunting look of, not knowledge, but understanding. And Eugene, as he sat at the table listening to Lenny describe the teaching life in America, smiled with *his* eyes.

Nicole, *Nee*-cole, Nicki of the gray eyes, was indeed watching Eugene from the window. Had been watching him all day, in fact.

She'd been watching a man with shaggy hair and a curious face that mocked her people, her world, a face that yawned with boredom at the manners surrounding her life; she watched a slightly slumped posture that suggested disbelief and a sense of bewilderment about the style of living that guided her thinking. Nicole caught snatches of conversation tinged with crisp subtle ridicule and humor; she reacted to a manner that vibrated sensuality, danger, warmth, and a pleading call to draw her into his world.

Nicole was a dreamer and she spent the day watching her dream function on her own lawn. In six hours, soon-to-be eighteen-year-old Nicole created her excitement, her seduction, her salvation, and of course, she fell in love with her creation.

It was as simple as that.

Eugene, the Savior, meanwhile, was starting to fidget out on the terrace. He tried to catch another glimpse of Gray-eyes, but she was hidden. He tried hard not to watch the coy exchanges between the young lovers nor the beaming expressions of the parents. Keeping only half of himself involved with his surroundings, Eugene drifted away into his own thoughts. He wondered why he was so full of disdain for what was nothing more than the most normal occurrence of a normal day in a normal life. Certainly he had seen relationships flower. He was not unaware of the joy that could be shared by intimacy. He was not even, he was sure, so cynically hardened and jaded that the niceties of everyday living were lost on him. And yet . . . and yet . . . he wished there were some way for him to intellectualize, at least to express, the pressure he felt smoking within him. Pressure that wouldn't allow life as it was to be embraced gracefully. Pressure that still sometimes struck him, spun him around, made him freeze in his tracks until he could clear his head and continue along his way; pressure that forced him to smirk and see it all simply as so (and goddamn, this was how shallow he was) *silly*. What a way to go through life. Thinking things were *silly*. Why? Why did he? Who knows? And who cares, when you get right down to it. Nothing sillier, he decided, than trying to figure out life's triviality. But some step was needed, some push must be given. He had thought that the move itself would have set him upon whatever the next plateau was. But he was wrong. Maybe there was no way up. Maybe you just were there. Ahhh. Well. Well. Was Willie getting to play in the Series for the Mets now?

"You will of course come, *non?*"

"*Pardon?*" Eugene had lost track of what he was of course coming to.

"Hélène's party. You will come, I hope."

A large French party. How nice. Lots of wine, women, and *chanson*. And dancing and philosophical discussion. Maybe Sartre will show up and play the piano or something. Uh huh. Sure. Relax. This ain't supposed to be the final retreat. This is *France*. Land of the grape. *La Tour Eiffel*. This is the change you were looking for. Maybe the next step. May even be a chance to sit on somebody's face.

"*Merci*, I would like to."

"It's done," said Henri. "*Bon*."

"Perhaps you can be Nicki's escort," smiled Hélène. Everyone laughed.

A week went by before Eugene received the letter. It was written in a dark blue ink, beautifully done by hand. Small and clear, with just the right amount of swirls. There was no salutation.

This will be a funny letter to receive, for you. It is a funny letter to write, for me. I followed you out into the garden the other day, after my sister and Lenny had gone off to talk and giggle and kiss each other. I watched you stroll and stretch and, from my spot in the bushes, I spied and watched you urinate on the grapevines. Papa was mad. I was not even supposed to leave my room, but I had to see you. Since I know all about you.

I watched you all day and saw that you were not like everyone else, not like *anyone* else. Don't ask me *how* I saw it, but I did. Truly. I see things like that.

This will most likely sound absurd to you, but now that I feel I know you, I can write this letter and surrender myself.

Yes, *surrender* myself. Are you laughing? I am, a little. But I have been waiting, my soul has been waiting, for something and someone. The people around me are fools, playing out their lives by rules and regulations I cannot recognize. You can't either, I *know*. I cannot fight them, these rules, these nets, these chains. But *you!* You are, you have. I *know!*

Please come and see me. I am not as foolish as this letter makes me sound. I feel that, perhaps, my life may at last gather meaning through yours.

In case you are wondering, this is not the way a typical French girl goes about meeting a man. Some of us are more subtle. But perhaps you wouldn't respond to subtlety. So this.
     Please.

                                        Nicole

Eugene put his head in his hands, on his face a smile that neither mocked nor celebrated, one that was simply there, and wrote back the following note to Nicole:

Dear Nicole,
Don't you even want to go to a movie first?

                                        Eugene

But he went to see her. Held out for three days and then just started walking. Started walking and suddenly found himself in front of the large house belonging to Henri and Elise Wickes. Nicole was sitting on the porch, draped in a chair, reading *Pamela*.

"Hello," he said. She looked lovely. Graceful. He found himself wishing he could paint, wanting to make her image a permanent one.
     "Hello," said Nicole and realized that in person he dazzled her. With his confidence and ease. With his fearlessness. His knowledge. With all that she knew about him and all she could never know. Then she said, "Excuse me," and started to leave.
     "Wait," he said. And she waited. "I got your note."
     "I know. I got yours." She blushed. A real blush. He smiled at the girl whose eyes projected such complete womanhood.
     "Please," Nicki said. "To come here just to laugh at me."
     Eugene stomped his boot on the ground and lit up one of his small Dutch cigars. Tobacco smoke and icy breath swirled in front of his face.
     "When I got your note," Nicole said, "I was never so unhappy in my life."

She looked up at him as if he should say something. He did.

"Let's take a walk. Yah?"

They walked and she wondered why he had come. She wished he would leave. She wished he would take her with him, but she knew he wouldn't, so she just wished he would leave.

"I wasn't laughing at you earlier," he told her.

"You were," she said.

"Well, maybe just a little bit."

"You think everything is funny."

"I think everything is funny."

"I think everything is sad," Nicole said.

"Well. We're probably both right."

They walked a little farther, Nicole nibbled on her right thumb. She reminded him of the children in the school-yard, but she was womanly, and she played with him like a woman. Eugene felt good. It was nice to walk, to talk quietly, to watch Nicole, to feel cold. He shoved his hands deep into his pockets while sauntering. Someone had a big fire going somewhere. It smelled okay. He flashed her a grin.

"So you watched me all day."

"Yes."

"Any worthwhile observations?"

"You look like you have money," Nicole said.

"I do."

"Do you like having money?"

"Yes. Do you?"

"No." She ran her hand across the top of her hair. "What did you do to get your money?"

"Nothing," he said.

"Me either," she said.

"Do you like doing nothing?" he asked.

"No," she said. "Do you?"

"Yes."

He watched her sway back and forth, watched her watching him.

"Why didn't you have lunch with us?" he asked.

She made a face, closing one eye, twisting up her mouth. "Why did you *come* to lunch?"

"I'm a friend of Lenny's."

"He's an idiot."

Eugene smiled. "I know."

"Then why are you his friend?"

Eugene shrugged.

"I don't have many friends," Nicole said.

"Why not?"

"I don't like people."

"That *is* a drawback as far as having friends."

"People are bad, I think, and they frighten me."

Again, Eugene just shrugged.

"They don't frighten you?" Nicole asked.

"Only when I think about them."

"I wish I could not think of them."

"It's easy," he said.

Nicole stopped. "My note," she said. "You thought it was crazy."

"It was."

"It was truthful."

"They're not mutually exclusive."

"I wish I were like your friend, Lenny," Nicole went on. "He brings his dreams to life so easily."

Eugene leaned forward, hands down on his knees, then arched himself backward.

And then something happened to his eyes. Something that happened on rare occasions.

They *softened*.

His mouth slanted up a bit on the left, his lips compressed. All reserve stripped away, all masks dropped instantly. And his eyes softened.

"I see such a strange combination of things inside you," she said. "And it's so hard to tell what's real and what isn't."

"Just assume everything's real," he said.

"And if everything's real, what matters?" she asked.

"Nothing," he answered.

They sat now. Nicole shivered and began covering up her legs with leaves, piling them high around her, pushing them away, starting again.

"You're not like your sister," Eugene said.

"No. Everyone can be put so easily into categories. Lenny is the dreamer, the liver of fables. Harmless. Ineffectual. Hélène is the manipulator, the predator, the twister of lives."

"What are you?"

"The doomed romantic pragmatist."

Eugene grinned. "And what am I?"

Nicole didn't grin, and said, "Whatever you want to be."

Eugene stood up, looked down at the sprawled figure, the large eyes, the long hair, the sad heart.

"You have someone left behind?" she asked.

"Never."

"Why?"

"I don't miss who I'm not with."

He knew that, if he wanted, she was his. She was offering herself, and trusting herself to him. He took her in, running his eyes from the tip of her boots, up her legs, which were curled under her. Her coat was open, he saw the ripples in her sweater, a brief flash of skin on the left part of her stomach. Her arms supported her, managed to hold her body off the ground. Her face showed that she was waiting expectantly.

He wondered if she were a virgin. He wondered if she were dependent on other people for love. He wondered why he dreaded getting to know her, feared familiarity, stayed away from what she had to offer. He wondered where her curiosity and her sadness would lead her.

Not to him, he decided.

He bent down, held out his hand, lifted her up onto her feet. Their eyes met, their hands held, until Eugene slipped away. She looked at him curiously, and he knew her eyes were asking him to stay, to help, to be what she wanted him to be. He looked at his watch.

"Goodbye," she said.

He nodded and watched as she headed down the path leading back to her life.

Nicole left Eugene in the woods, blowing smoky breath out to warm his hands.

14.

Nicole hadn't seen Eugene for three weeks. She'd called him, written notes, but he refused to respond. Several times she walked by his house, standing a little ways off, leaning against a tree by the side of the road, waiting only to catch a glimpse of the unwitting ghost haunting her eighteenth-century mind. Perspiring despite the wind and the cold, she would suddenly be seized by strange new sensations of awkwardness and ugliness, self-doubt and insecurity. She would see that her shirtsleeve was too short and that her wrist looked too bony. Or that her hair had matted against her forehead and looked dirty. She would stand waiting to see him, hoping to confront him, yet afraid and vulnerable and half-hoping that her longings stayed separate from reality.

Now, on the day before Hélène's party, Nicole stood brooding, staring out her window, seeing only an endlessly gray landscape.

Around her, the house was lively; there were people rushing nervously around preparing for the following day. Nicole stayed removed, a phantom in the background, listless and

vacuous. As night glided past her window, Nicole turned
away. She stepped slowly and deliberately out of her loose
nightgown, feeling the silk delicately lace first her shoulders, then her arms, then breasts, belly, hips, thighs, and
ankles. Nicole flung her hair up from the back, dropped her
hands by her side, walked to her bed, and slid under the
sheet. With only a sliver of moonlight outlining a green
glass vase, the girl tossed and turned, felt queasy pains in
her stomach, and finally fell asleep.

Nicole dreamed.

She dreamed she was walking across a snowy clearing. A
desolate field, gloomy and dark. Eerie gray foam seemed to
pour over her vision.

Moving forward, Nicole crosses a bridge, a swaying tres-
tle. She snaps a twig off of a tree, dropping it into water
bubbling and boiling below. The bridge begins to shake and
Nicole panics, spinning in every direction, her mouth dry,
her chest heaving, finding nowhere to run. No escape.

Suddenly, a huge shaggy animal appears out of nowhere.
An indeterminate species, lumbering, awkward, unstoppable.
He picks up the terrified girl and carries her across the
bridge. Setting her down on the other side, the animal offers
her his powerful hairy paw. Opening her mouth in a silent
scream, Nicole refuses help from the ugly horror. Without
looking back, she runs, faster and faster, trying desperately
to outrun this beast loping tirelessly after her. Back in the
snow, Nicole races through the woods, branches and thorns
lashing at her, ripping her skin, tearing her clothes. She
slips and slides, her skin dampens, freezes. She runs until
she is exhausted, until her strength gives out.

Nicole falls forward, pitching into the white slush. Breathing hard, gasping, she collapses. The creature is there, curious, timid, strong. He picks her up and carries her for
miles, careful not to jostle her, to his home, a stone castle,
cold and lonely.

They sit at a table with monsters. A deformed dog, a
dwarf with a pig's face, a half-horse/half-snake, giant in-
sects. Wild animals sit at attention, eating with knives and
forks, murmuring too low for her to hear, too fast for her to
comprehend. They wear suits and ties, and some of them

stare intently at a television set which blares out an American western.

At the head of the table sits Eugene. With a huge fur coat, that bloats his body, pulled around him, and with his long flowing hair and beard, he radiates an aura of early civilization, violence, of chivalry, of armored power about to be carelessly unleashed. Eugene picks up a huge silver goblet, drinks down gallons of wine, the red liquid dripping from his mouth, streaming, glancing off the table, spreading on the floor.

A hard cold wind blows open the front door and all the wooden shutters. The light, hundreds of thick candles, disappears. Nicole shivers as she is plunged into darkness. The monsters around her begin beating the table with the silverware and their hands. They stomp on the floor and begin to scream and spit, ugly noises coming out of their mouths. Overwhelmed by their sudden odor, Nicole faints.

Eugene grabs her before she hits the ground, silently leading her away from the disgusting creatures, the clamoring monsters. Eugene and Nicole disappear into a small room. With a fireplace permanently ablaze. And giant pillows. There are decanters of wine and brandy around, long mirrors, wooden chairs, and silver jeweled daggers on the wall. Eugene moves toward her, taking off his coat. He wears a loose white shirt that he pulls over his head. Nicole sees his ribs, his body hard, lean, muscular. Eugene reaches her, stretches out his arms. She leans in to him, his arms cover her, one hand grabbing the back of her head, stroking her hair, pulling her into his chest. They kiss, break apart. Nicole steps out of her shoes, her long dress, her underwear, and stands before him naked. Eugene smiles, calls her Nicki, and they are both naked, embracing, loving. His body feels firm and strong. Warm and smooth. She is perfect, with hard breasts and a thin stomach, legs that wrap around him and clutch him inward. Their eyes meet and she sees, for the first time, that his eyes express his soul, and that his soul is loving, tender, all-desirous, and fearless. As he grips her, wanting her, and as Nicole spreads herself for him, Eugene easily moves his body on top of her and prepares to enter.

The door to their isolation is thrust open, a man hidden by shade lurches in and moves toward Eugene. Eugene is up and, with the fluid motion of a fighting warrior, swings his arms around to rip a dagger off the wall and lash it out toward the intruder. The man is sliced, he reels backward. Eugene, as if choreographed, whirls again in slow motion and pins the man against the wall. He raises the dagger and snaps it downward. The man is dead. Eugene kneels over him and cuts out his heart.

Nicole screamed in her dream and in her blue-gray room in Sancerre she woke up wet and hot and terrified.

"Are you all right?"
It was a sleepy and cautious Hélène. She stood by the foot of Nicole's bed.
"Yes."
"You yelled out."
"Yes."
"A bad dream."
Nicole nodded, her throat dry and bad-tasting. Hélène looked concerned, sat on the edge of the bed.
"What were you dreaming about?"
Nicole could only shake her head twice quickly and pull up her knees, wrapping them with her hands, laying her cheek on the left cap. She looked at and was comforted by two volumes of Walter Scott and Byron on her night table.
"I wish we had things to talk about, Nicki. But we don't."
Nicole smiled, a wisp of a smile, and shook her head again.
"I'd like to know what gives people bad dreams," said Hélène. And she lay down next to her sister to fall asleep.

When Nicole awoke around dawn, she was alone. The first rays of the morning filtered in through her curtains. There was a pleasant chill to the fresh day and Nicole embraced it fearfully. Tired. Troubled. Thankful that the darkness kept her secrets safe.
As usual, light came and the day wasted away for Nicole. She hung by the curtains in her room, her sunken eyes

searching the landscape, her trembling psyche longing for peace.

Her searching and her longing found no relief. Her world remained a dim shadow.

For Henri and Elise and Hélène, the day glowed. There was a party.

The first guests began arriving in the late afternoon, and by six-thirty the house was nearly filled. Henri didn't scrimp on this affair. Over two hundred guests had been invited, nearly all accepted. Local friends, business contacts, far-away acquaintances of long ago, friends of friends. Painters and carpenters and wine merchants. Catholics and Jews and Muslims, fat dancing aunts and stunning slim mistresses. It was something to see.

Only French businessmen can appear casual in gray suits and thin ties; only French women can pull off wearing too dressy, too sexy clothes at an inappropriate affair. And there were fifty or sixty of Henri's Parisian friends whose clothes were wrong but whose manner was right. They relaxed in the country, immediately slowing down, the men assuming an air of condescending sophistication, the women measuring the countrified sex appeal, taking care to lounge carelessly, their jewelry jingling. Cigarettes dangled from lips, glasses tilted down over the ends of noses. Wine was sniffed appreciatively. Delicate arms were tanned by southern sun and only the miracle of a powerful *savoir-faire* kept jackets draped loosely over shoulders.

The country folk were up for a good time. Dancing and singing and lots of drinking. A big mouthful of turkey and a *baguette* along with a chance to stare at and maybe grab a bit of Parisian thigh. Most of the local women wore loose-fitting frocks, a little too short or a little too long. The girls were younger-looking than their years, the women older-looking.

French women are sexy: they have style and even those, the majority, who are not beauties, have that curl to their lip; that smoothness to their complexion; that walk; that look in their eye that shows innate style, a sense of humor, and a glowing innocence combined with the knowledge of a good

fuck. There definitely is something about *les femmes fran-
çaises*, and at Hélène's party the something was charging
through the air. Crackling. Sizzling. Perhaps, en masse, it
amounted not to sexual electricity but rather a sense of
event. Perhaps the French sense of history can create it.
Maybe it was just the wine. But as Lenny and Eugene
walked into the party, it appeared that all heads turned. The
music stopped just at that moment. Conversation ceased.
The only sounds, so it seemed, coming from two hundred
people, were the clinking of glasses and the chewing of
food. Lenny, ever-oblivious to any crucial action, lifted his
head and went to search out the birthday girl, a fawning
look of bemusement immediately enveloping his face. Eugene
sized up the party in its instant freeze-frame, blinked, turned
hesitantly back to safety, then was pulled into their midst.
He made a most unwilling Jonah.

Henri came up and kissed Eugene on both cheeks. Elise
took his hand and pecked at his beard. Hélène, bombed
already, holding on to Lenny, hugged him. Nicole, dragged
over by her father, grimaced wanly and held out a limp
hand. Her stomach rumbled, her knees were weak, her de-
meanor was timid and demoralized. She turned away at the
first opportunity, grabbing the arm of Monsieur Paul Luce,
the forty-six-year-old Parisian whose presence as an escort
had caused her to sulk and bitch three weeks before. She
cast a glance back at her white knight, who dropped his
eyes in irritation and looked through the girl as if he'd never
seen her before. He rubbed his eyes with one hand.

Eugene had made a mistake. A big one. He shouldn't
have come, and he realized it immediately. The second he
walked in he was put off and upset; his manner lost its usual
casual bounce, taking on a grim stiffness, a reserved disgust. His contempt was usually flip, almost attractive for the
subtly masochistic mass psychology. But now it wasn't flip.
It wasn't light or cynical. For one brief moment something
else dominated him and leered out from under the years of
protective facades—and it was ugly.

Eugene covered it up, his mask replaced itself almost
instantly. But there it was, and he was aware and he was

startled. He was not in control. His eyes narrowed and his lip curled and his face hardened. And his self was no longer a removed observer. It was a grotesque participant.

He started to sweat when he realized something was very wrong.

To draw his mind away from this momentary unveiling, Eugene set it to taking in the party. He concentrated on each person milling around, coming to some sort of caricaturing conclusion about each of them. The mask worked, covering him up temporarily, and Eugene took a deep breath before smiling through his teeth.

Nicole was the first victim of his perception. She practically leapt into his line of vision as he walked in the door. Eugene hated what he saw. The comic high tragedy, the swoons, the look of longing despair. The pain. Shit, it was the pain Eugene hated. It was the pain he wanted no part of. It was the unnecessary pain that he caused inexorably, that reversed itself, riveting itself onto Eugene, widening his eyes, lowering his tolerance for human contact.

There was, lurking somewhere deep within Eugene's consciousness, an overwhelming urge to ease other people's pain. Because he'd never really felt any, not the way others felt it. Cut him physically and he'd bleed. Wound him emotionally and he'd only regenerate. And it would make his life so much easier if he could only put the world out of its misery. It would, at least, make the world much less unpredictable, much less vindictive. Much less dangerous.

At one time, Eugene thought it was fear of death that motivated the craziness he saw around him. He learned differently, though. That it was rather, a dread of pain. It was not mortality that spun the world, it was the *vulnerability* of mortality. But Eugene had never felt particularly vulnerable. Because pain, he knew, like everything else except life and death themselves, ultimately wasn't real. And what wasn't real, he thought, couldn't hurt.

Obviously, he was wrong.

Hurt was all he saw now. Beneath every exterior, lying low in every human soul, he sensed fear and hurt and pain. And what he, as a child, had perceived as funny and strange behavior, had seen as a teen-ager as crazy irrationality, had met as an adult as despairing meaninglessness, he now saw only as naked, raw, energized pain. And where he once saw such emotional human products as love and compassion, he now saw only self-produced pain, a race of beings bent on self-destruction, evident in the subtlest of everyday actions and going all the way up to the awesomely apparent workings of the nations of the world. A world that had moved along for thousands of years, progressing only through its own unreal pain.

And it was the pain that he wouldn't look at as he turned his glance away from Nicole, keeping himself fascinated with the floor until she was busy dancing with some old fart wearing a ringed neck scarf.

Ah yes. He had wanted a change and one had come. Eugene wasn't sure what delicate shifting of balance had gone on inside him. Only that all the events, the people, and the thoughts of his life had somehow added up to where he was, who he was, and what he was thinking and doing and being now.

Eugene sure was surprised.

When he looked up, other faces glided before him. Physical deformities, unpleasant aberrations sprung upon him, assaulted his senses before anything else. Obesity, dwarfishness, chubby thighs, big noses, funny haircombs, bad breath and body odor; awkward dancers, stupid eyes, pantlegs that were too short to cover shoes that were the wrong color, anyway. Eugene suddenly found himself in the center of a bad Channel 5 Saturday-morning cartoon. The people danced around like cartoon silverware, the servants grew big platter-lips and rolling melon-eyes. Conversation squeaked in the background. He could almost see a mouse trying to carry the food off the table on a stretcher, a cat rushing along, screeching, only to wind up with a sledgehammer blow on the head, flattening him like a pancake. Eugene shook his head as if to clear away the nonsense, but it didn't do much good. He realized that people were talking to him, he tried hard to concentrate. Nothing was making very much sense, but no one seemed to notice, and his incoherent mumbling passed as conversation. Eugene realized he could have been anywhere, with anyone, and there would be no difference, no change. And he realized something that left him momentarily dazed and devastated: As most thoughts were born in pain or in exaltation, he had little to say to anyone because he found life so dull; there was nothing to be said about it. Words attempting to glorify or even make life interesting were nothing more than attempts to justify existence. Something he never deemed worth justification. As he stared in stunned silence, he thought, perhaps the perfectly adjusted organism *should* be silent. Maybe it's only through silence, beyond the fatuous clamor, that one can be still enough to stumble upon the silence of which the Universe is made. And lost in his stumbling, Eugene felt dubious, the thought occurring to him, as he watched his view of the world scurry around in front of him, that he was not a successful human being. He had created a personality, he had even, to the best of his knowledge, explored his limitations, and, in some strange ways, managed to control his passion. But as his silent moment passed, as he slowly melted back into the reality of the party, he felt he should have been working at something else the whole time. And he suddenly felt reborn and strong and he felt triumphant as suddenly he understood why people drank and danced and partied till they were ready to drop; why mankind married and went to Cleveland to visit relatives and created the electric can opener; why there were wars and countries and laws and jobs and prisons and sports and art. You had to take it out some way or other, your passion, or it just ate you up.

Eugene knew no, it wouldn't.

And he wondered why he was cursed with this relentless drive to fulfill his passionate desires instead of, like the world, being content to ease them out of his existence.

And he knew no, he couldn't.

And then he looked right through himself and he saw what he was. And like a snap back from an acid time distortion, Eugene looked around the room, as if searching for an old familiar face, a way back to reality. There was none.

What there *was*, were a few people who noticed Nicole's histrionics, her discomfort, and realized that it was due to Eugene's presence.

"That bastard," somebody grunted. "He really *is* a bastard."

But that awareness was limited to the few sober people who bothered to pay attention to the electricity in the air. Most of the others were too drunk. And it was no wonder. The lure was too great. The feast was incredible. Worthy of a Homeric comparison.

Liquor flowed in what seemed to be a constant stream, a continual communal wrist that turned slightly, almost on command, to cause all liquid to disappear as quickly as it could be produced. Henri had supplied his two hundred with his private wine stock, the Lafites, Margaux, Latours, and Haut Brions. There were bottles of whiskey, of liqueurs, of cognacs ample for a Roman orgy. The food was almost gross in its sexually bursting appearance. Game and beef and cheese, meltingly ripe, succulent fruits with bread that was torn to shreds and potatoes mashed by fingers, dripping from beards around the room. Hands glistened with grease, teeth shone with food particles between them. Gluttony is one of the most satisfying of the seven sins and one of the more necessary. For it helps to ease the pain of not participating in the other six. But as Eugene stepped toward the spread, he felt something start to move within him. He closed his eyes and tried to shut off his brain. His anger was no longer a part of him. This was something else, a something even more incomprehensible, more terrible and, he felt, potentially more dangerous. He grabbed a turkey leg, bit into it ferociously, and poured a glass of fifty-nine Mouton-Rothschild down after it. His eyes flew around the room as he nervously wondered what was going on. And what the next step was.

Soon, Henri began to toast. Basically a good man, drink and emotion made him sentimental. After singing the glories of his wife and eldest daughter, he turned to Nicole and praised her to the skies. His remote beauty, his mysterious and independent love. His daughter whom he wanted to devour with deeply felt love and protection. Nicole became even more discomposed and embarrassed. She happened to catch Eugene's eye and his funny look which she saw was, at least partly, an understanding look about her predicament. He knew. Nicole became ecstatic and turned happily away, practically floating over the highly polished floor. Eugene *did* know, but his knowledge had soared past Nicole, reducing her to nothing. He saw, was distracted by, her sudden change in mood. Eugene swore under his breath and went for more wine.

The party continued. People disappeared in small clusters. Eugene got very drunk. Nicole stared after him. Some of the guests started to play charades. Hélène strolled by, without Lenny. She asked Eugene to dance. He, eyes blurred, looked her over carefully, nodded his agreement, and as a slow song started up, held her close, moving in time to the music.

"Where's Lenny?" he slurred.

"Don't know. Off reciting poetry somewhere, I imagine."

Eugene raised his eyes appreciatively and grunted.

"Where's my sister?"

"Dunno. Off *sobbing* somewhere, I 'magine."

It was Hélène's turn to enjoy a bit of alcoholic wit.

"Happy birthday, by the way," Eugene said.

"Thank you." Her cheek brushed against his chin, her eyes blinked sexily at him. "I didn't think you would really come."

"How could I stay away?"

He rolled his eyes and she yelped. They danced. Then her lips grazed his neck. He could just barely feel the tip of her tongue. Then the music stopped, people crowded by, Eugene reeled a few degrees backward. Across the room he could see Lenny staring at them over a conversation with two drunk old men. Eugene, as he whispered something in Hélène's ear, making her laugh, could sense the gut resentment and curious sense of confusion that he knew Lenny was feeling as he watched their shallow intimacy. Eugene looked at Hélène, who, he saw, had pretty much decided to fuck him, and despite everything, perhaps because of everything, Eugene felt a twitch of excitement and let himself be swept along with it. His eyes closed for just an instant, a split second of concentration, and then he decided yes, yes. Yes. He put his hand on her hip. She hesitated then ran a finger over his knuckles. Eugene decided that he'd like nothing better than to get locked in a niner with Hélène, and he looked down at a mammoth boner just as Nicole came by, nervously trying to catch his attention.

Nicole was very sober. She had tried to get drunk, but nothing went down her throat. She had spent most of the evening talking or dancing with Monsieur Luce, who was very nice and obviously wanted her, but was very dull and old and polite. As she watched Eugene lean on her sister, Nicole flushed and began to fantasize about going over to Eugene, leading him away, and fulfilling his every sexual desire for days then weeks then years then forever. She squirmed at the combination of excitement and degradation he aroused in her, completely lost herself in her world of made-up sexuality. Her face took on a glazed look of passion and she was a million miles away, a retreat into the courtly world of *Moll Flanders* and *Joseph Andrews*, a world updated to include the fuck-and-suck touch of *Deep Throat* and *Screw* magazine.

What she did, when Eugene was through dancing with Hélène, was, instead of blowing him, to ask him if he would dance with her.

"Not now," he said.

"Oh."

She waited.

But that was it.

She saw in his eyes one of those I-Can't-Believe-You're-Still-Bothering-Me looks, along with a curious stare, wondering what more she could have to say. Then his eyes moved on past her, searching for . . . it didn't matter what . . . searching for someone, something else. She stuttered out another "oh," then her face fell and the weight in her heart sagged her shoulders and took away her power of speech. She stayed in front of him for a few more seconds, awkward, feeling foolish. Nicole turned and fled upstairs to be alone with her ray of moonlight.

Eugene, moving assuredly toward his only reality, saw Lenny monopolized by those around him, took Hélène's arm, and said, "C'mon."

"Where?"

"Outside."

They walked about fifty yards away from the house. Eugene, striding intently with his hands in his pockets, was breathing hard. It was freezing cold. When they stopped walking, Eugene stepped toward Hélène and kissed her—not a soft, lingering kiss of affection but a hard, sloppy kiss with sucking noises and legs rubbing together to further any sense of contact.

"Come," she said, half-gasping, half-hiccuping. "To the greenhouse. It's warm."

Eugene, not having bothered to put on his coat, shivered, and they ran to the old glass building. Eugene kept his eyes on her, an appreciative yet self-satisfied sort of smile on his face. She looked so wild and so inviting, so dangerous and so willing. So French. So unbelievably fuckable. It was awesome. Between that thick, sexy accent and her clinging dress. He could see her nipples and feel her warmth, make out the tight lines of her body, catch her litheness and strength as they ran. And whatever it was that started to overcome him earlier at the party, now erupted once and for all, spewed out as he couldn't wait any longer and lunged at her, not bothering even to search for the light, pulling Hélène toward him. He bit into her lip, causing her to cry out and draw away. She scratched into his back, taking blood away underneath her nails, and wrapped both her legs around him, grinding herself into his body. Eugene tore at her clothes, pulled them from her till she was completely naked. Fumbling a bit with his belt buckle, Hélène finally undressed him, licked her lips, and climbed onto him.

Writhing on the dirt and carpet of the greenhouse, Hélène sat on top of Eugene, leaning way over so she could kiss him, lick him, rub her breasts over his chest, smother him. She moved hard and purposefully, up and down, digging and forcing him in and out. She groaned, started to fall off him, exhausted, but he grabbed her, straightened her out, made her keep going. Eugene was silent except for his heavy breathing. His hands held her perfectly smooth ass, gripping, fingers up her hole, and he shoved himself back and forth mightily, urgently. He could feel the sucking acceptance of him within her, the secure confines of filling her entirely. As if one body, they locked themselves together in animal movement. The familiar gyrating lacked all pretensions, all motivations except immediate fulfillment. In a pounding rhythm, they continued, and Eugene, teeth clenched, pouring sweat, skyrocketed into the knowledge that this was his release, this was his absolute freedom from the dictatorial commands of his lust. This must be his moment, his all. This was his last remaining instinct, his only exposure, his truth, his justice, his reward. His very being. And he looked up into Hélène's brown eyes, her gaping mouth, her hanging breasts, and something was very, very wrong.

He was *thinking;* mental images bounding back and forth between visions of Nicole hurtling up the stairs, Lenny eyeing him suspiciously, the people at the party trying to gobble and slurp up their own despair. He heard inane babblings from his present as well as screams from his past. His throat tightened as his mind drifted away from his body to peer down at his absurd actions instead of, as always in the middle of an exhilarating sexual experience, merging and melting together to form a sensual calm.

Physically, he responded; mentally, he withdrew, his eyes narrowed, he could feel himself moving away, removing himself from any sense of participation in what was meant to be his own salvation. As Hélène came, dripping down upon him, and as Eugene came, spurting up into her, Eugene pulsated with the realization that his one touch with the force of the Universe was now broken. He wanted to shake the girl and force her to keep moving, force his wild appetite to clutch and claw for more, for nonstop gratification. He wanted to throw his arms back and scream of his power, of his might, of his never-ending strength. But suddenly it was over; he faded and all was still.

All was still.

Drained, Eugene held the girl tight to stop her squirming. He was left to his own empty self; the sweat broke out in torrents.

"You're perspiring," she noticed.

"Uh," Eugene breathed. He wiped his forehead but it didn't do any good.

The stimulus ended, he was searching for more. He was unmoved. Unfulfilled. Afraid.

Eugene was bored.

Collapsing, sobbing with exhausted pleasure, Hélène now rolled off of him and curled up in a corner. Eugene, shaking slightly, drew his arms back, stretched naked on the ground, turned his head slightly to the right, and saw, through the fogged window, Lenny, friend and poet, the sorrow of a shattered world etched onto his features, staring horrified at the sight of human satisfaction.

15.

The music from the party strained through the glass windows and slipped under the crack in the door. It sounded so distant. The muddled, incoherent party conversations came across as so alien. Eugene, his breath coming in short bursts, lowered his eyes for just an instant, then craned to get a better look at the spot where he had seen Lenny. There was nothing now. Only the stir of the wind and a branch banging monotonously against the roof.

Eugene lay with his neck thrown back, arms crossed over his head, legs apart and bent. Eyes closed now. His mouth was dry and his dick was wet, little bubbles of sperm occasionally appearing and dripping onto the hair on his stomach. All strength disappeared from his body, a pleasant and peaceful lifting of an unwanted burden.

Hélène slowly uncurled herself, walked to peer out the window. It was very dark, the lit windows of the main house emitting a fuzzy brightness thanks to a now-heavy fog wrapping itself outside the party. She turned back to look at the shadows of the plants within the greenhouse. They hung over the aisles, drooping sleepily. Warm and protected from the outside.

Without putting on her clothes, Hélène bent over from the waist, touching her toes in an exaggerated stretching motion. She flattened her palms against the floor and kept them there, twisting her head to look at Eugene.

Our man hadn't moved much. His arms covered his eyes, though he was watching the girl in front of him. What he wanted to do was get out of there as soon as he could. He wanted to beat it immediately.

Hélène moved languorously to sit down next to Eugene. She tossed her leg over his chest, twisting her ankle to rub up against him, then bent forward in an embrace. Her hands smoothed over his torso, nails lightly scratching over his muscles. She kissed his neck, nuzzled his cheek. He reacted not at all, arms never unfolding, eyes sternly blank. Hélène had the glow of a beginning around her. Eugene, with no response to her affection, had the vacant look of an ending on his face.

They said nothing. No movement. No tender glances or smooth reassurances. Eugene was a million miles away, and his boredom, within fifteen minutes, spread to and consumed Hélène.

She fidgeted, she coughed, she lay still and then began drumming her fingers on his chest. And lit a cigarette. She began to regret what had just happened as she began to hear the familiar noises of the disbanding party. Turning her thoughts to Lenny, deciding she wanted Lenny with her now, Hélène ran her fingers through her own hair and silently hated Eugene for being such a disappointment, for making her feel so meaningless and unreal. For treating her, for seeing her as if she were only a tiny cog in an unimportant machine.

Eugene got up slowly and dressed. He looked at her for an instant, said goodbye. Received no response.

"Got a croissant?" he said.

"What?"

"I once thought all French girls carried croissants with them."

"No."

"Oh."

He stepped outside, headed back to the party to get his coat from one of the servants, drove home, and went straight to sleep.

On the second floor of the Wickes house, as sweeping and cleaning and refrigerating were going on below, Nicole stood staring out the window, now a familiar and comfortable pose. Slowly and deliberately she breathed in deeply of the cold night air, pleased, despite herself, to feel the tingle of goosebumps skitter over her body. Her thoughts were as dark and as black as the starless night.

She heard the opening and closing of drawers, the rustling of blankets and sheets, slippered footsteps. The sounds of her sister preparing for bed. Earlier Nicole had watched when Hélène came back to the party, listless and disheveled, noticeably lacking her usual taunting gaiety and burning control of every situation. Nicole had seen her looking for Lenny, had also seen Lenny storm from the party in a burst of frenzied tension. Nicole had watched carefully for Eugene, had seen him stroll in after his absence, slip on his coat, and saunter out the front door. Watched him hesitate and carefully move his eyes across the party.

For one brief, exciting moment she was sure he was searching for *her*, and she moved to take an impulsive step toward him. But she stopped, frozen, when she saw his eyes and what was in them. It was a haunting look that almost knocked her over with its distaste, its horror, its total disavowal of the humanness of its owner. She was sure he saw her, sure that his eyes screamed out for her. But before she unfroze, he was gone. A figure in an old English movie lurching out of a doorway and disappearing into the fog. Alone.

Eugene had made love to Hélène, Nicole knew. Couldn't miss that expression on her sister's face when she returned. Nicole *knew*, and as she heard the scratching of Hélène's toothbrush, she tried to piece together the evening, making an honest if gentle attempt to probe her fragile mind.

There was nothing but that one glance he gave her, that look of understanding and appreciation for her situation that came early in the evening. That was what she was going on.

That was what she was positive must fester beneath his uncaring shell—knowledge. And Nicole really and truly believed that with knowledge came the ability to love and love deeply and absolutely. She religiously held on to the belief that knowledge *is* love, and that wisdom and comprehension created an insight into a universal human soul of kindness and decency and placid passion. She was going on that one glance, yes, but there was also that other—when Eugene gritted his teeth at the door to try and hold back his fear of the human condition. His fear that he had been mutilated beyond recognition by that condition and its all-encompassing past and present. It was that look that Nicole could not comprehend. It was that horror that she now rationalized away as sentimentally and romantically as one would make excuses for a date showing up late. For as things stood, Nicole had no other choice.

Now Nicole, her bare feet curling on the icy wooden floor, could hear Hélène crawl into bed. She wanted to go to her sister and hit her and beat this new secret out of her. Why had Eugene picked Hélène, why had he succumbed to her superficial charms? Why had he chosen to devastate his friend, why to so resolutely avoid *her*, Nicole, who would so willingly subjugate herself for his desire? Why was he passing her by? Why did he function as he did, why did he hate, why did he *know*, why did his image crawl under her skin and threaten to burst her open? Nicole wept by the window, Hélène moaned quietly in her bed.

Eugene was sound asleep at home.

He awoke late the next morning, having spent an uninterrupted night. He squinted and shook his head as he woke, his mouth filled with the familiar morning-after taste of dry cotton and muddy boots. A cracked note escaped from his throat, his head fell back on the pillow for a few dreaming seconds. Then he sat straight up, opening himself up to the morning cold.

It was too early in the morning for him to have *thought* yet. Nude, he slowly and steadily guided himself downstairs, poured himself a wineglass of orange juice squeezed in daily quarts by the cleaning woman. He sniffed and drank some of it, his tongue spreading it over his cracked lips, then carried the juice back upstairs as he walked into the bathroom, setting the glass down on the porcelain sink.

Eugene, though he was alone in the house, closed the door to the bathroom and turned on the shower. Scalding hot water thrust downward and the room filled with steam. Eugene stepped into the bath and stood under the hot torrent, letting his body relax, drooping his head, surrendering himself to the heat and the warmth. He didn't move, letting the water pelt him full force, his mouth open, his eyes closed, his hair now plastered back, his chest heaving. After maybe fifteen minutes, he slowly raised his arm and turned off the knob. Then, staying where he was, watching the drops from the showerhead trickle slowly down, Eugene let the water drip from him, twisting his body and raising his eyes, his first real awareness of the day.

Stepping out of the shower, he now picked up a towel, drying first his hair then running the cloth over his body, standing in front of the steam-clouded full-length mirror. He methodically began to wipe the fog off the glass with two fingers, making a not-unpleasant squeaking noise. Eugene peered into the mirror, clear, reflecting glass once again, as he inspected his body.

His hair was slicked back and still long. Dark. Thick. Curly. His beard was short, trimmed professionally, but full. Eugene ran his fingers through the beard, twirling the short hairs, carefully noting the different colors of red and brown that seemed to streak it. Eyes moved downward now to his chest and upper arms. There was more black hair on his chest, and he placed his right hand over first one then the other breast, feeling the small bumps, the tiny imperfections, a slight scratch from an unknown source. Arms were thin but hard. He smiled as he found himself searching for a ripple of muscle.

Making a fist, tensing his entire body, Eugene now let his gaze slip down to his stomach, a faint bulge, a slightly flabby roll beginning to appear. Down to his waist and still visible ribs. He could see his penis hanging down. Not really all that long or thick. Balls not too large. Lots of hair. He picked up the tip in his hands, running his fingers up and down. He got a very slight hard-on and grinned, marveling at the fact that it was this relatively small and ugly piece of wrinkled flesh that moved his world, dominated his every action, controlled his very life. He gripped it tighter, felt it grow hard, then limp again. He scratched his balls.

The cold outside air was now coming through to the bathroom, beginning to break the mood of the shower, as Eugene continued his visual odyssey. Hard thighs, knees that were twisted slightly and off-center, calves that had to be described only as nondescript. He would never know his calves from anyone else's and didn't really care to.

Eugene now took in his long neck, skipping over his ankles and feet, blinked at the mirror, and peered deeply into his own eyes.

They were bloodshot. And there were lines around them. Eugene thought they looked a little sad, a little tired. A little fearful. He couldn't detect any desire in them, any lust. Any humor. Any of the things everyone else seemed to constantly react to. He moved his face to within an inch of the mirror and reached back into his mind, desperate to find *something* emanating from his eyes, preferably something that might propel him high onto the level of reality he was seeking. As he stiffened his right arm, running his left hand over the muscle, Eugene heard a loud, hard knocking at his door. He turned his head, hesitated a second, and then moved to get a pair of jeans and go confront his visitor.

Lenny, when he woke up early that morning, had two things on his mind. A powerful desire to forgive Hélène and an overpowering urge to hurt Eugene. To hurt.

He awoke with a bitter taste in his mouth and it wasn't from too much alcohol. It was, to his mixed-up mind, the taste of disillusionment and disgust and of shattered romance. The poet greeted the day a crazy man. Tried to eat and couldn't. Attempted to write, found it impossible. Paced. Pounded his fist into the wall and gave out low wails. His eyes projected the agony of a wounded animal.

Unable to keep his misery pent up alone any longer, Lenny went over to see Hélène. His stomach was cramping, rumbling ominously, and he felt a bit nauseous, but he had to go. Had to get this fury out of his system. Words— comforting, soothing, logical words could, he hoped, ease

the pain, at least shift it over to Hélène. Get it out of his
stomach and into her brain. And then he would forgive her.
Finding her ashamed and humiliated, he would open up his
arms and make things clean again. She would repent. He
would console. This was love, Lenny knew, and love could
work miracles.

When he saw her sitting by the window, he almost vomited
as the vision of the night before floated in front of him.
Lenny staggered in the pathway before composing himself,
straightening up and forcing his body to go forward toward
the house. His hands shook when he used the knocker on
the front door and his eye began to tic. But yes, he was
ready to forgive her because he knew she was feeling pain
greater than his. Pain that would wrench tears out of her,
bring forth words of devotion. God, as she opened the door
he hated her, and couldn't wait to take her in his arms and
forgive her.

When Hélène opened the door, she smiled. "Hello,"
she said.

Lenny froze. She was glad to see him.

"Come in," Hélène said.

He didn't say anything. Felt nauseous again.

"I looked for you last night," his angel said, "but you
were gone." She took his hand. "You left early."

Lenny tried to swallow. Impossible. "I . . . I left . . ."

Hélène pushed back her hair and kissed him lightly,
taking his other hand. Lenny left both of them with her
limply.

"Look," he said. Very quietly. "I saw you."

"Pappa just woke up," she whispered. "People stayed
till dawn."

"Uh."

"*J'étais* bombed. I was very drunk."

"I saw you."

"Where?"

"I saw the whole thing. God*dammit*!" And Lenny swung
his fist through the air with enough force to spin his body
around. Hélène said nothing. She watched him carefully.
Out of the corner of her eye she saw Nicole standing at the
top of the stairwell. A spooky kid, she thought. So terribly
silent.

"Do you understand what I'm telling you?"

"Yes," she said.

"So?"

"I knew you'd come back."

Lenny burst out crying.

"Oh, Jesus, don't start crying." Hélène took his hand again and wiped his tears away with the back of her hand.

"I feel," he gasped, "like someone just kicked me in the stomach."

"It's done."

"I *know* it's done!" He was yelling finally. Then he sobbed and caught his breath. "Can I have some water or something? I don't feel so hot."

"Sit down next to me," Hélène purred.

"No. You don't understand."

"No."

"I *came* here!" He lashed out and kicked over a table.

"Lenny, don't, for God's sake!"

"I came here, all the way here. I love you. I made *plans*. I mean I *thought* about this. My whole life and everything."

"Yes, but that's *you*. That's not *me*."

He stood straight. Absolutely silent.

"Lenny."

He stared at her pleadingly, hoping for the words that would clear away his misery.

"I was drunk."

"No!"

Now she spoke very quietly. "If I had it to do all over again, I wouldn't."

"You wouldn't?"

"But I might."

Lenny looked past Hélène at Nicole. She returned his gaze coldly, pityingly. Henri Wickes came into the room in his robe and said hello to Lenny, who bolted out the door, ran to his car, stopped driving halfway home to cry and shout, bang the steering wheel, and throw up.

Lenny went back to where he lived, the cozy little room upstairs in the house belonging to the Sancerre baker. He nervously strolled around the house, sat down and wrote furiously. Stanzas and stanzas of angry poetry, poems of

rejected love and shattered bliss and the treachery of mankind. He wrote for hours and drank a lot. Even smoked a
few cigarettes that the baker's wife had left lying around.
The poems, as he reread them, were forced and bad. Strained.
Unsure of themselves. Reaching for superhuman rage and
grasping only self-pitying insecurity. Lenny tore them up.

At one in the afternoon, alone in the house, he went into
the baker's den, marched straight toward a small hutch by
the bookcase, opened the third drawer down from the top,
and took out two pistols.
Then he sat down and wrote one short page.
Then he went out again.

And there was Lenny as Eugene opened the door, hair
wet, naked except for a pair of faded jeans. They faced each
other in silence until Eugene coughed. Then he squinted and
turned disinterestedly back inside, expecting Lenny to follow. When he realized that Lenny wasn't behind him, Eugene
half-turned his head toward the door. Just in time to see
Lenny take the baker's gun out of his jacket pocket, aim it
across the room straight at Eugene's heart, and pull the
trigger.
He missed by three feet but the noise almost gave Eugene
a heart attack. He was in motion before the shot was fired,
rolled backward into the living room, hiding behind an easy
chair.

"What the fuck are you doing, you asshole?"
Lenny raced around to his right and fired the gun again,
this time putting a bullet into the wooden floor. Eugene dove
over the couch and lay there panting. Neither moved nor
said anything. Eugene wet his lips, decided he felt like Peter
Sellers playing Quilty to Lenny's James Mason's Humbert.
He wondered why he couldn't even feel like Quilty, only
Peter Sellers. He didn't have time to come up with an an-
swer.
"You can stand up now," Lenny breathed.
Eugene, on the floor, was searching for a poker or a lamp
to grab and throw at the lunatic.
"Stand up, Gene. I won't shoot."

Eugene stood up very slowly and Lenny shot again, this time aiming for Eugene's head but doing nothing more than shattering a window. Eugene threw a chair at the would-be assassin and made a wild dash up the stairs. Lenny missed again as Eugene vaulted the top of the railing and closed himself into his bedroom. Safe for the minute, he looked down. No fucking locks on the door.

So he waited. Panting, pressed up against the door with all his might, he waited and listened. Nothing. His breath returned to a normal pattern. The muscles in his upper arm were contracting. Eugene concentrated on stopping them. Couldn't. Then they stopped on their own. He sagged a bit. Not terribly frightened now, he sagged with the absurdity of the situation, allowing a shaky grin to rest momentarily on his lips.

"Gene?"

Eugene didn't answer. Tensed his body again.

"Gene. Listen. Ah have two guns heah. Ah could kill you if Ah wanted."

The thing to do, Eugene knew, was to stay calm and outwit him. He opened his mouth, determined not to lose his cool or to sink down to Lenny's level.

"Yeah. You're a great shot, you fuckin' asshole!"

Oh well. Eugene shrugged.

"Heah's what Ah'm gonna do, though."

Nothing from Eugene's end this time.

"You listenin'?"

No answer.

"Well, what Ah'm gonna do is get ridda one o' these bullets. Listen."

Eugene heard a shot. No question about it. He jumped instinctively at the noise.

"That leaves me one bullet in each gun. Y'understand?"

"What the fuck are you doing?"

"We'ah gonna have a duel."

Oh Jesus, Eugene thought. He *is* a total lunatic. How could he not have known Lenny was a lunatic. Jesus Christ! *Everybody's* a fucking lunatic if you just give 'em a chance.

"And don't worry, Gene. Heah. Look."

A piece of paper slipped under the door and Eugene almost hit the ceiling at the unexpected sight. Calming himself, he bent down, still pushing awkwardly against the door. He stopped before he touched the paper.

"Didja read it?"

"What does it say?"

"It says it's okay if somethin' happens to me. Says that Ah broke in heah and tried to shoot you. It's a confession."

"Very noble."

"Thank you."

"Lenny."

"What?"

"Can I ask you a question?"

"Yeah."

"Do you have any idea how crazy this is?"

"Ah'm gonna ask you somethin'."

"Yah."

"Do you know that's the first question you've evah asked me?"

Eugene took a deep breath.

"Uh . . . Lenny."

"What?"

"This is not gonna get you in solid with Hélène."

"Doesn't matter now."

"Why?"

"Because it's over."

"Jesus, all I did was fuck her."

"You ruined her! I saw."

"She doesn't even *like* me. What you saw was just a drunken fuck!"

"What *I* saw was someone who I'd never touch again because you made her repulsive. You killed her, in a way. You killed me."

"Oh yeah. That's right. I must have missed something at the time."

"Open the door, Gene, and I'll give you the gun."

"I can't believe this."

"Open the door."

Eugene opened the door a crack. Nothing happened. He opened it some more. Barrel first, a gun was slowly handed in to him. Eugene took it, sliding his hand around it, then grabbing and yanking as hard as he could. The gun clattered across the room and Eugene sprawled after it. He grabbed it and rolled up with the gun pointed straight at the door. After a few seconds of standing in his gunslinger pose, Eugene wiped his hands on his pants and waited for Lenny to do something else.

"Come out into the hallway, Gene."

"Chuck them guns in the creek."

"What?"

Eugene shook his head, laughed to himself and then completely relaxed. Something went out of him.

Since the moment he was born, there had been nothing but input except for an occasional sperm ejaculation. That was the only thing that was ever released from his insides, put forth into the world. Until now. When everything that had ever piled up inside him flooded away in one instant.

"Nothing," he said.

"Then come out into the hallway."

Eugene cautiously kicked the door open. It creaked. He hesitated and then he dramatically stepped into the hall, one large stride, back straight, head cocked back. Lenny stood there, arms hanging down at his side. He was a mess.

"You fucking madman," Eugene said.

"Yeah."

Lenny moved back several paces, his hands shaking, his veins sticking out in his neck. He screamed out, one inconsolable, desolate shriek, jerked up his gun, and pulled the trigger.

There was an absolute silence as Eugene heard the bullet splinter into the wall behind him. He turned to look at the hole, at the ragged pieces of wood that were just beginning to float to the floor. Lenny quivered slightly, body twitching in spasmodic jerks. There were tears that he wiped away with his sleeve.

Eugene started to say something and then he saw.

He caught Lenny's face as it tilted up to stare at him, and Eugene saw, one more time, the look of unendurable pain on someone's face. A look that stemmed from the man's very soul. Pain that was stamped indelibly in those eyes, stamped by Eugene's very being and *only* by his very being.

"Tell me," Lenny said. "I have to know."

Eugene saw the hatred that he produced, the turmoil he

created, the absolute and devastating pain that surrounded
him, suffocated him, and forever tried to tame and destroy
him.

"Now that we're alone. Now that there's nothing, no one
to interfere. You have to tell me. I have to know."

Eugene understood.

"I want things to make sense," Lenny said. He was
crying. "You make everything wrong."

Eugene knew what Lenny wanted. What everyone wanted.

"If only you were wicked. If only you could close my
eyes and bring me back what I lost." Lenny's words seemed
to come minutes apart. They made no sense to Eugene. He
knew what was inside Lenny, but all that was getting out
were sounds. Raw, jumbled sounds. Too slow, too deep.
Cracked. Unintelligible.

"Iffff . . . ohhhhnnnnlllyyyy . . . wwwwhhhatttt . . .
IIIII'vvveee . . . lossssstttt . . ."

Behind Lenny was a mirror and for the first time, Eugene
noticed his reflection. He looked great. His hair had somehow fallen into a tousled order, coming down over his forehead, curling up just before his shoulders. His stomach was
sucked in, his chest was out, heaving. His face was stern,
impassive. And, he knew, uncaring. He looked different
than he had looked just minutes before. He saw something
in his eyes. Saw something glitter, something spark, something smile at him, Eugene looked at Lenny, but saw around
him, through him. Saw himself.

"Tell me, Gene," Lenny was saying. Or at least Eugene
thought he was saying, for the words now were one with
Eugene's thoughts. They were the questions he'd asked himself once, many times, no longer. They were all the thoughts
of his past, all the yearnings, the confusion, the emptiness.
Suddenly it was the voice of Mort, and then of his friends,
and then of all the women he, Eugene, had known, and then
the voice of everyone demanding, asking, pleading, beseech-
ing, lying, screaming, dying.

"Have you deceived everyone," the voice said, "for so
long that you can no longer reveal yourself? Or is this it?
Are you really so simple, so bare? So ugly? Have you
discarded good and evil by choosing them out of existence?
Are you forever in action for the future or are you lost in the

philosophy of the past? Are you an answer, are you real, or are you an incredibly destructive lie? And what are you afraid of? Tell me, please," Lenny said, and he was having trouble breathing. "Is the strength you possess the strength of passion or the strength of despair? And can either one last for a lifetime?"

So Lenny tilted forward now to hear Eugene's answer. He gritted his teeth and strained his eyes and waited for Eugene's explanation. He waited for the myriad complexities that tortured, ruptured his soul, to be dissolved. Lenny waited for those magical eyes to produce, at long last, the promised secret. And Eugene knew. Yes, he knew. Lenny wanted the secret of choice; and the choice was between truth, righteousness, and holiness on one side, and lust and base propensities, obscure passions and perdition on the other. And Eugene felt his breast opening, splitting, and he felt his self being wrenched, ripped, stolen from his body. And he looked at Lenny, and at the pain, and at the world, and he thought, ah, if only they could understand that there's no difference between the truth of a poet and the raging passion of annihilation.

One more time Lenny said, "Tell me," and their eyes met. Then Eugene closed his. And for the first time in his life Eugene had a way to eradicate the pain he found in others, to destroy the unreal chains that were endlessly lashing out at him. A way to escape the reverberations of people's fear, to finalize the meaninglessness of this omnipresent suffering. He opened his eyes.

And Eugene looked down, then surely and collectedly raised the gun that Lenny had handed to him. He held it out, toward Lenny, put both hands together around it. Eugene aimed carefully, gently eased the trigger back, and fired.

A large chunk of Lenny's head and a lot of very red blood splattered against the carpet and the wall and a lower corner of a window. Some of Lenny's hair stuck to the blood on the mirror behind him and his body flew backward and to the side, collapsing, draped over a small antique end table like a pile of old clothes.

Eugene rocked backward. He went up on the balls of his feet, balanced himself, then came back down to stand flat-footed. He chewed on his lower lip, took a long, inspecting look at Lenny's mutilated face. Those clouded eyes betrayed, no longer pain, but death.

Eugene's eyes blinked.

Out of the muck and mire, pal, was all he could think. Be thankful it's over, that I did it for you, instead of waiting for time to tear you apart. Maybe you *would* have served the ages with your words and idealism and your love. Most likely you would have altered and deserted beauty in the face of your pain. You would have worn it in comfort, lived in the suburbs, might have learned that life is shabby at the bottom. You might have grown too bored to think. Had gout at forty. Turned fat and flabby and worn slippers while you ate and drank. You might have gone to bed and died while doctors hemmed and hawed, while women sobbed and ate chocolate. You might have lived like everyone else, lied your way through sixty years of facing up to your humanity.

Well, he thought. Well. Don't worry about it now. You're outta the club.

Eugene knew that winter was now well into its stay. He walked into his bedroom and pulled on a shirt, trying to stem the cold tide icing his body.

16.

In the winter, in France, the desolation melts with the snow and celebration comes with the spring thaw. The vines renew their inebriating cycle, tables are filled once again outside the cafés. Clothes peel off and flesh opens up both to the sun and to the excited tourists who come to France in the spring to learn about life and watch the exposed bodies.

Sancerre was no different. Some things changed over the winter, some merely stayed hidden to resurface, some just outright died.

Lenny's grave was in a cemetery right outside of town. It was a small burial ground, filled mostly with men killed in World Wars I and II and families that had spent their entire lives in the village. Lenny's body lay under a nondescript stone. Though all around flowers covered the dead, there was nothing brightening the spot where it read

Leonard Latimer
1951—1974.

Lenny's barren grave was the only visible refusal to acknowledge winter's end and spring's beginning.

For the first month or so, Hélène came regularly to the
gravesite. She wore black—she looked terrific in black—and
she would, twice a week, stand over her dead lover, place
fresh flowers on the ground, and let a tear slip down her
cheek.

After the first month, Hélène's visits were less frequent.
Once a week at the most. And then once a month. And then
she met a thirty-four-year-old Parisian lawyer who helped to
ease all sense of guilt and obligation, and she ended her
visits.

In early March, less than four months after Lenny's
death, Hélène married and moved to Paris. Love, like
everything else, proved itself steeped in mortality.

Eugene, thanks to Lenny's note and the obvious evidence,
was found innocent of any legal wrongdoing, innocent of
everything except honorably defending his own life. He left
Sancerre, though, as soon as he was cleared. Just disappeared.
Told no one where he was going. Most of his possessions
stayed in the house, which remained vacant and ghostlike.
As far as the town was concerned, all traces of his existence
disappeared when Eugene did.

Except for Nicole, of course.
Nicole mourned Eugene still, haunted regularly by his
past actions as well as by her own imagination. She
brooded, she lost weight. Her color faded and her actions
were listless and spiritless. Once, while brushing her long
hair in front of a mirror, she found herself crying, for no
apparent reason. She jumped up, wiped her cheeks dry, and
stood in the middle of her room, helpless. She didn't
understand what had happened or how things had gone so
wrong. She was not prepared for scenes in real life to be so
incomplete, to vanish, in fact, before their proper end.

Nicole, too, was leaving Sancerre. She was being sent
away to Paris, to continue her education and to wipe clean
her slate. To make her a character in a different play.

This day was her last in her hometown. Summer was to
be spent with Hélène and with relatives, preparing for

school and the fall. And she strolled, on her last day, over to
Eugene's vacated farmhouse. And she walked up the front
path, opened the door, stepped inside.

Very little had changed, although someone had been
keeping the place clean. The furniture was all as it had
been. Unburned logs still waited by the fireplace. Half-drunk
bottles of liquor stood on the bar. Any trace of the violence
that had transpired, however, was long since scrubbed
away.

Nicole passed through the front of the house, sat down,
leaned all the way back on the couch. The cushion sank,
then held firm. She waited, stood up because she felt
Eugene's presence too strongly. She felt he was there, she
could see him, his eyes. So she stood up and kept moving,
hoping that movement would keep her own private ghost
from overpowering her. She glided into the den.

Nicole looked over the books Eugene had left behind.
She thumbed through a few of the more worn volumes as if
they, perhaps, were responsible, or could, at the very least,
explain.

Not once did it occur to Nicole to blame Eugene for what
had happened—to Hélène, to Lenny, to her. She was
already wise enough never to blame the catalyst for the
reactions to his initial actions and emanations. But she
would not allow herself to realize that all initial actions and
emanations result from choice. If he acted in ignorance it
made him only purer in his ethereal sensuality. If indeed he
acted from knowledge, it made him more powerful, more
godlike. Anyone, Nicole knew, could be good if they willed
it. But to be like Eugene required genius.

Nicole imagined many times the scene of Lenny's death.
She knew it centered around Eugene, conceded that her
loved one was the driving force behind the tragedy. She
knew that was the reality of the situation. But Nicole also
recognized that Eugene did not really belong to reality. Yes,
he was aware of it, had contact, rushed around within and
fought his way through it. But he was beyond reality; it was
not a sufficient stimulus for him.

Nicole picked up a book of matches off of a bookshelf.
Lit one, let it burn, blew it out. She remembered when she
had heard the news about Lenny. The police had gone

straight for Lenny's landlord, the baker, who had assumed the role of next of kin. Shocked, sick, the baker had rushed straight to the Wickeses'. Only Nicole was home.

"Mademoiselle," said the baker, "may I come in?"

Nicole, of course, ushered him inside. The baker fidgeted and paced and took her hands in his own.

"There is no end to tragedy," the man had told her, and Nicole nodded agreement, believed him, without knowing why. "The young man has been shot."

She thought Eugene was dead. She had underestimated human hatred, thinking it capable, at its strongest point, only of focusing outwardly. She saw Eugene bloody and disfigured, so she fainted. Nicole was out for just a few seconds, because she opened her eyes and saw, through her haze, the baker, gently slapping her cheeks. She could feel the sweat from his palms slide off him onto her, roll down to her neck. The next thing she remembered was Hélène and her mother bursting in. Hélène was crying, she knew, and Elise was trying to calm her down. As soon as Nicole was able to discover the truth through the screams, the cries, the hysteria, she ran upstairs, locked herself in her room, and smiled savagely. Rocked back and forth on her bed thinking only that Eugene was all right, that Eugene was alive, that Eugene was still there for her.

As soon as she was able, Nicole slipped away to wait for him. She stood on his porch, *stood* there, unmoving, for an hour. Then she leaned against a post, then dangled her legs off the railing. Then sat. She waited through much of the night but he never came.

The next day Nicole was there early, at Eugene's house. She stood guard for hours, for the entire day. The house seemed empty; it was dark, quiet. A tomb. She tried to get in; the door was locked. She peered in the window, tapped on the glass. Knocked on the wooden door. The police came by; she didn't speak to them. She walked away.

The third day she knew he was gone. Somehow he had slipped by her. Had disappeared. Nicole didn't know what she was going to do.

She did things, of course. Mostly the same things she always did. Now she was doing something in Eugene's

house, while he was long gone, and she was preparing to
disappear also. To Paris.

Nicole walked into the dining room, went through the
kitchen, peeked into the pantry. She climbed up the stairs,
examined the hallway. She went into his bedroom.

On a round table, underneath a double window, lay a
book. A notebook. It was closed.

Nicole's eyes were immediately drawn to it, her body
swayed toward it. She knew what it was. What it had to be.

Nicole knew it was his writings. She knew it was his
thoughts, that it had been left for her; that it was a solution,
an explanation. That it was his legacy, that it would be the
truth, an unveiling, a sharing, a merger.

Nicole gripped the tabletop, weak. She caressed the
cover of the notebook, gently, repeatedly. It was hard and
the bottom half, which had been in the shade, was cool.
Nicole trembled. She opened the book, ready to flip delicately
through the sagacious insights of a mind she knew would
never allow itself to rest. On the first page there was an
epigram.

> No wonder of it: sheer plod makes plough
>   down sillion
> Shine, and blue-bleak embers, ah my dear,
>   Fall, gall themselves, and gash gold-vermillion
>   —Gerard Manley Hopkins: *The Windhover*

Nicole turned to see what followed. There were more
quotes.

> The fact is, it seems, that the most you can hope is to be a little
> less, in the end, the creature you were in the beginning, and the
> middle.
>   —Samuel Beckett: *Malloy*

and

> When one ceases to feel, I am of the opinion one should keep
> quiet.
>   —André Breton: *Manifesto of Surrealism*

and

> The only way to behave to a woman is to make love to her if she is pretty, and to someone else if she is plain.
>
> —Oscar Wilde: *The Importance of Being Earnest*

She picked the book up and ripped at the open pages, turning them faster and faster. There were more epigrams, other people's words. More distillations of people's thoughts.

> Matter rather than forms should be the object of our attention, its configurations and changes of configuration, and simple action, and law of action or motion; for forms are figments of the human mind, unless you will call those laws of action forms.
>
> —Francis Bacon: *Novum Organum*

and

> What a profound harmony controls all the components of history, and that even in those centuries of history which seem to be the most monstrous and the maddest, the immortal thirst for beauty has always found its satisfaction.
>
> —Charles Baudelaire: *The Painter of Modern Life*

More thoughts that somehow when seen naked, seen removed from their whole, separate from their proper entity, were . . . different. Distorted. Perverted. Wrong.

> . . . faint or loud, cry is cry, all that matters is that it should cease.
>
> —Samuel Beckett: *First Love*

and

"Oh Jake," Brett said, "we could have had such a damned good time together."

Ahead was a mounted policeman in khaki directing traffic. He raised his baton. The car slowed suddenly, pressing Brett against me.

"Yes," I said. "Isn't it pretty to think so?"
—Ernest Hemingway: *The Sun Also Rises*

and finally

I suspect people of plotting to make me happy.
—J.D. Salinger: *Raise High the Roof Beam,*
Carpenters

Nicole counted the quotes, spread out over the first few pages, then closed the book. Slammed it shut. She was trembling and she leaned against a wall, her back fitting into the corner of the room. She opened the book again. She turned past the quotations, still fearless, put her thumb and forefinger on the top right corner of the notebook and turned to look at the rest of Eugene.

There were one hundred and sixty-five blank pages.

17.

Eugene, in his first trip to Paris, had written to Casey:

If New York is the electronic center of the world, Paris is definitely its existential source. When walking in Paris it is necessary to have one's eyes open constantly, to strain to take in every odor, every crackle, every smile, and even then it's impossible to contain Paris. The Tuileries burst into the open and the Champs Elysées broaden, stretch magnificently and powerfully, disdainful of the traffic and the tourists' cameras. The doors of the apartment houses beckon, the black elevator cages invite mystery and intrigue. The aromas whip the senses like glorious wisps of smoke; the colored liqueurs, the flesh, the gambling, the coffee, the shops, the stands, the language all assault as one, offering to be understood and appreciated, sniffing intolerance and pity. Caressing, stroking, removed, indifferent. Yes. New York is a persistent intruder, a fighter always moving forward, a never-ending and never-relenting reminder of beauty and ugliness. Paris is beautifully, deliciously, gloriously indifferent.

There are endless ways to describe Paris; it's a city for adjective lovers. But there is only one way to *feel* it. That's to find a side stairway leading up to Montmartre, preferably around sunset. Climb the steep steps, then up the winding cobblestone paths, looking back occasionally to keep track of the vanishing city. Ascend, past the little Van Gogh houses, past the Matisse restaurants, up, up, until the square, with its junk painters and whistlers and guitar players, and then past even that till the Sacré Coeur looms, white and cold. Then stand in front and look past the leather vendors and jewelry salesmen, past the sidewalk chalk artists, past today, and there's the city. In its totality. A sweeping view of l'Opéra and l'Arc de Triomphe and la Tour Eiffel. A stark and perfect canvas, an illumination of more than mere beauty. It's music, is Paris. It's a love song. It's the overpowering past making its presence known the only way it can.

Gray-eyed Nicole Wickes, in her remorseful stupor, saw nothing of her ride from Sancerre to Paris; she certainly didn't hear the strains of the city's instrumental lure. It was a short trip, and for most of it she kept her eyes closed. Just outside the city, an American accent turned her head. It was a young backpacker who smiled at her when her eyes flew open. He was drinking wine out of a *bode* bag, and he offered some to her. Nicole didn't acknowledge his gesture; she turned to stare out the window. She saw a scattered herd of sleeping cows and then the city began. A few small, modern houses clustered together. Then a few more. Then a factory and tall buildings and then Paris. Nicole didn't notice the rooftops, the unmistakable grillework. She didn't notice the glistening Seine, blue and smooth. She didn't notice anything until the train slipped out of the sun and into the dark, easing into the station, the gare de l'ouest.

The American tried to help Nicole with her luggage, speaking clumsy French, trying to be engaging, but she ignored him. The train ride made her feel dirty. She stood alone in the compartment and fluffed out her hair. She saw her reflection in the train window. Where one of her cheeks should have been, there was a porter, motioning her to come off the train.

There were the usual station noises and smells that bombarded her, but this time she fought them off, and before she'd taken three steps she had turned the transient excitement into a static blur.

Nicole got into a taxi outside the station, gave the driver

Hélène's address. The driver checked the girl out via his rearview mirror.

"Hey," he said to his passenger. "Do you know Paris?"

"Yes."

"So how can you be sad?"

He pulled up in front of an iron gate, through which was visible a handsome courtyard and a stately three-winged building.

"My dear girl," said the driver. "I see a young woman walking toward this cab as if she is the person you are supposed to meet. I see, too, that you happen to be crying. That is not the most pleasant way to greet an old friend. May I give you some advice? And I will make this quick since your friend is gaining on us."

Nicole nodded, embarrassed.

"You are very young and I assure you that whatever has already happened to you is nothing compared to what *will* happen to you. Which isn't really cheery, I'm aware of that. But the thing is, eventually you become too old even to cry. So now . . . enjoy even the tears. That's all."

Hélène opened the back door of the cab and kissed her sister on both cheeks, warmly. Nicole sniffled and gave the driver a big tip and went in through the iron gates.

Hélène's apartment was very special and the room that Nicole moved into was a charming one with curved windows and a view of Montmartre. But her second day there, Nicole told Hélène she wanted to move to the vacant maid's quarters.

"The maid's room, Nicki?"

"*Oui.*"

"*Mais, pourquoi?*"

"Because I like it."

Most old French apartment buildings have a top floor with tiny rooms built originally for household servants, usually occupied now by *au pair* girls. The rooms are usually not well kept up. This one had no running water. There was one toilet to the floor. The climb was endless and steep, and once up, the immediate reality was the isolated cubicle and little else. Hélène's husband, Gérard, wouldn't hear of the move at first. But Hélène, who knew better than to try to understand her sister, talked to him and told him about Nicki. He looked at the younger girl closely and patted her on the head and said she could certainly have the room.

Nicole smiled for the first time since arriving in Paris.

She did the cooking, most of the time, for Hélène and Gérard. Hélène hated to cook. She liked to dress up in tight dresses, cut low to reveal, to push out her wonderful breasts, and go out to dinner. Nicole liked the kitchen; she liked to slice things. She enjoyed the whole cycle of turning something raw and harsh into a seasoned, delicate, consumable whole. She appreciated the order and discipline of preparation, and she always arranged the table settings as if they were integral theatrical props, always the same, always perfect. She loved the moment when all was on the table, steaming, before the first bite destroyed, before the devouring began. She was a creative cook but also a simple one. A gentle chef, she was.

Nicole chopped and broiled and spread and baked for several weeks. And read and sat in her room. And hummed while she looked out the window. Waiting. Which was her decision. She decided to wait.

She met a few people. Saw a circus, her first. Caught her first Bertolucci film. Engaged in pleasant chit-chat with Hélène's friends. Nicole never wavered. When her need for physical contact started to keep her awake at night, she seduced a boy she met in the Parc Monceau. Brought him up to her room, had sex with him, twice, waved him away.

Nicole was becoming beautiful. She gained a few pounds, her body rearranged itself a bit. She exercised to keep fit, and danced. When school started, students and teachers stared at her and tried to meet her and tried to penetrate, alternately, her emotional and physical shields. She was taken out to shows, to nightclubs, drinking. She delighted in their attempts, let them all think they were doing very well.

School was fine. Her life with Hélène was pleasant. Her circle of friends was nice. Her cultural activities were stimulating. Once, after Nicole had been in Paris for four months, Hélène's husband tapped at her door, sat on her bed, smoked his cigarette, and made conversation as Nicole stared out the window. "Nicki," Gérard asked her. "What is it you . . . ah . . . seem to be waiting for?"

Nicole smiled.

And waited.

It was September. Eugene had been traveling, had been away from Sancerre for over ten months.

His departure had been a rather sudden one. The French police were as anxious for Eugene to leave as he was to get out of there. The investigation took exactly three days. They discovered Eugene in his living room, calm, expressionless, quietly finishing off the remains of a bottle of Courvoisier. Lenny was exactly where he had fallen, the blood drying quickly and caking, his color fading, disappearing forever. The police had Lenny's letter of confession, noted the overturned furniture, checked out the baker's missing guns. They asked Eugene to go with them. He drained his glass, shrugged, and went.

An hour later, he started to cry.

At first it was quiet sobs, so they made no move to silence him. He sat on a cold, wooden bench, shivering, unable to control irregular spasms in his arms and back. His neck twitched and his mouth opened and he cried the silent, harsh bray of a baby. Then he started breathing hard and then he started screaming.

The police told him to be quiet. Eugene screamed some more. Piercing, anguished wails punctuated by long periods of vomiting, tears falling at such a rate as to actually produce small puddles on the chair and on the floor.

The police told him that this was all a formality, that they could see he had been attacked by a madman. They told him they knew he was innocent. Eugene continued to scream and cry and vomit.

They told him to go home and wait. He went home and waited. In the dark. In silence. He sat upstairs, hardly moving except for the heaving of his chest and the slow but steady grinding of his jaw. Once, twice, maybe several times he heard faint knocking at the front door, scratching at a window or two. But he ignored them. Just sat and cried for three days, and then he was declared a free man. The police told him that he would probably be better off leaving the country. Eugene cried and that night he left the country.

He cried for two weeks, practically every waking minute. Sat alone in cafés dripping tears into his whiskey, splattered the marble floor under Michelangelo's *David*, stained the saddle of his rented burro. He wept in his hotel rooms, while coasting in gondolas. He cried till his throat threatened to close up and his sides heaved with pain.

He just cried his fucking guts out.

And then he stopped.

It was while he was in Amsterdam. Watching an old man building a cabinet on the street. Hammering and sawing, fingers scarred from infinite miscalculations and incalculable moments of carelessness. The old man looked up to see Eugene. He flashed a toothy grin, pulled his black wool hat farther down on his head, and went back to his carpentry. Eugene looked up and down the canals to see a civilization of builders and tinkerers and people who seized things and shaped them to their own liking. Made things useful. Women who nursed large families, made their own clothes, swept their own chimneys. He saw whores who realized they were nothing but scantily packaged meat, so displayed themselves accordingly in windows. Men caught their fish, cut them up, and went out on street corners to sell off their catches. They went into bars and got drunk, sobered up, slapped each other on the back, kicked around a soccer ball, stoked up a wood stove. He saw people who didn't seem to mind life, just went about their business, just got things done then woke up and did them again.

He saw people whose lives were devoted to survival, plain and simple.

He stared blankly at the cabinetmaker, then blinked. Blinked away an alternative, blinked away a civilization. He stopped crying and went to London.

He stayed in London a while, a couple of months. Took *bawths* and had his tea in the afternoon. Became very civilized, dining at Inigo Jones and Rule's, going to sleep early, standing to the right while riding the escalators. Rowing around the Serpentine, strolling Park Lane, stiffly perusing the *Guardian*. Taking in the theater and nibbling cucumber sandwiches. Saying "bloody" when he meant "fucking."

And when he thought he was going to start crying again, Eugene left London. Went to Stockholm. Flew directly.

Lived in the Old Town. Hit a few discothèques, bicycled, drank beer, stroked blonde hair and comforted himself one night at a time inside athletic thighs.

Moved on.

Kept moving.

Soon, he never felt like crying anymore. He never felt like anything anymore.

And somewhere along the line he *stopped* moving. He was aware, distantly, that he had to return to New York eventually to take care of financial matters. So he drifted that way, slowly. Getting sidetracked sometimes but getting there. And then he just stopped. Ran down. Didn't even drift. He froze. In some city. He didn't leave because there was nowhere he wanted to go. He didn't want to stay where he was because *wherever* he was, it was the same as anywhere he'd ever been. Not only didn't he know what to do, he didn't care what he did. He didn't think, he didn't react, he just stopped moving. And somehow he found himself in Paris. He looked up and there he was, at night, walking along a side street off the Place Pigalle. He was surprised. There were beautiful women, sexy, half-naked, sitting at a bar, in the dark, a strange red glow hovering over but never touching their bodies.

Then Eugene was at a table, a booth, and two of the whores came over to him. One sat opposite him, a tall, dark-haired, exquisite-looking woman. She wore a halter top and a fringe skirt. The other one, an Oriental, sat next to him, on top of him. She put her hand on his dick, stroked it, pushed her breasts into his face.

"How much?" he asked.

"One thousand francs for both," one of them said. "Two hundred dollars."

"Okay," said Eugene.

The girl across from him slid under the table. She spread his legs apart and massaged both his legs.

"Here?" he said.

The Oriental took one breast out of her shirt. She put the nipple in his mouth. Her breast was hard, firm, strong. She pushed it around his face, over his eyes, slowly, cradling, happy. She took off her shirt, placed both breasts on his lips and moved them sideways, back and forth. She poured champagne over her breasts and into his mouth.

The girl under the table unzipped his pants and was kissing his penis. Her tongue was incredibly long and she licked him. She stopped, grabbed his hand and, though he couldn't see, knew that she had him fingering her cunt.

The Oriental was completely naked now. And she was on all fours, her ass pointed in his direction. She was giggling and pouring champagne over her whole body.

One girl was giving him a hand job, hard jerking motions. Then both were kneeling, blowing him. One wrapped her legs around him, then one sat on his lap and tried to stick him inside her. Then they both stopped laughing.

Eugene wasn't getting hard.

They worked at it, moved faster, more seriously, started to sweat. They really went to work.

They started to mutter to each other, then to him. He nervously drank more champagne. He got limper.

They blew out exhausted breaths, he pushed them away and zipped himself up. He gave them an extra hundred dollars. He stood up. He walked out of the bar.

Out on the street, he felt feverish. Sick. He kept wiping his forehead and nervously rubbing his eyes. Some people stared at him, he looked up, saw blurs, felt self-conscious.

Eugene tried walking. He bumped into someone. A woman. He looked down. At Nicole.

"Hello," she said.

"Hello."

"How are you?"

He closed his eyes.

"Fine." It came out as a whisper.

"What have you been doing?" Nicole asked.

And Eugene struggled, forced himself, miraculously managed to put the smallest smile on his face.

"Oh," he said. "The usual things."

Before he even asked, she gave him her address and phone number and took his. She disappeared. He went to his hotel, took a bath, a long one. He lay down in bed, on the cool sheets. In her maid's room, Nicole stayed awake. She was smiling. He was back. She thought he looked wonderful. She had waited. And he was back. Things had come out the way she knew they must. Right.

She called him in the morning and they met for breakfast.

"What would you like?"

"Strawberries." Beaming.

"Yes," he said. "Good." Recovering.

She was rubbing one finger lightly over her lip. She was basking. Soaking luxuriously.

"I knew you'd come," she said.

He smiled at her.

"I spotted you a few days ago, you know," she said.

"I didn't know."

"Oh yes. I've been following you for two days. I didn't have to take your address last night. I knew the hotel and your room number."

"Why didn't you speak up earlier?"

"I enjoyed following you. Watching you. I like watching you."

"Well," he said.

"You're different," she told him.

"Than what?"

"Than what you were. You look like . . . I can touch you. Reach you now."

"I'm no different."

"Yes."

"Why?"

"Because I *think* it."

"And that makes it so?"

"Yes."

"Nicki, Nicki, Nicki," said Eugene. "Will nothing ever change you?"

"Nothing."

"Don't let me."

"Change?"

He shook his head. "Change you."

"No," she said.

They parted for the afternoon but met for dinner. He took her to Lasserre.

"So how's school?"

"Please!"

"What?"

"I wish you'd take me seriously."

"No you don't."

"What?" she said and then, "Oh," when she remembered Lenny.

"Plus de vin?" the sommelier asked.

"Oui," Eugene answered. *"Une autre bouteille."*

They drank it slowly.

The next night he took her to a little bistro all the way east. They took the Métro to Mairie de Monteuil and walked a few blocks to the restaurant. There were only two other customers, and the owner greeted them warmly.

"Bonsoir, m'sieur, dame."

They each ordered a *kir,* and then the owner's wife came over to the table.

"Bonsoir, m'sieur, dame." And then to Eugene she said, "Welcome back."

He smiled and she went off to bring them some special pâté.

"How do you know this place?" Nicole asked.

"The way I know everything."

"Yes. And how is that?"

"Somebody told me," he said.

Dinner was superb, and afterward they went to a jazz club in the Latin Quarter. Down into a *cave,* descending a steep stone stairway until a bar magically appeared, and music. A big band was wailing and everyone was doing the swing. Nicole laughed and ran onto the dance floor, her legs already moving double-time. Eugene, slower, behind her, looked the place over, took in all the young dancers, all the beer drinkers, all the talkers. The music stopped, then a new song started, a fast one, and Eugene was movin' those feet, sliding Nicole from side to side. They danced and they laughed till late, and got fairly drunk. Out on the street, Nicole fell into his body, throwing her arms around his neck. He smiled and hailed a cab, dragging her after him, and he dropped her off at home. Eugene then had the driver take him back down to his hotel. He lit a cigar and watched Paris go by. The back window was open, just a few inches; the wind felt good.

They met again the next afternoon. To shop and look in windows. And to tour. They went to the top of the Eiffel Tower, which Nicole insisted was ugly. And then they walked along Avenue Georges V and above the Tuileries, in and out of the stone archways. They walked all the way north, almost to Clichy, then circled back to find themselves near Nicole and Hélène's apartment.

Nicole lived in the seventeenth arrondissement, and her special shopping street was the Rue de Levi, which she loved, so that's where they went. It's four blocks long, and first they passed a fruit and vegetable stand. And then a café where Nicole said they made wonderful cheap ham omelets. After that a *patisserie,* and then just row after row of sausages, cheeses, and pastries. Different, wonderful pâtés. Small, thick quiches. Chickens and ducks and rabbits hung by their feet. Stuffed mushrooms, salads, *pain au chocolat* and *tartes aux fruits* subtly made their presence known on the street. Colors darted back and forth as tomatoes and carrots and yogurts and Perrier bottles were tossed around, swung about in wicker carrying baskets.

Eugene and Nicki bought some camembert and bread and small tomatoes and pears and a liter of milk. They strolled to the park across the Rue du Rome, sat on a large rock, and attacked their food. Eugene had to force the milk open, some of it spurted, getting onto his fingers. He laughed. Nicole tore off a piece of bread with her teeth.

"Jesus, look at you," he said. "Look at you eat."

"I'm hungry."

"You're gonna eat your knuckles."

"I'm not." She tossed her hair back indignantly and shook it. "Usually I am more refined."

"I bring out the beast in you, huh?"

"No," Nicole said, and she put her cheese down on top of a smoothed-out paper bag. "I know what you think of people, I know how you judge them. But I think I can do things and say things around you and you won't care. You won't judge. I don't know why that is. How can you stand so apart from people, yet participate so fully in their everyday actions?"

He was surprised by her question. So he actually gave it some thought. "It's because nothing makes any difference to me," he said.

"No. It's more than that. That's not it."

"Yes it is."

"I see such love in you."

"You're about the only one."

"It's there."

He half-laughed, half-shrugged. Started to say something. Stopped. "What makes you so sure?"

"Why else would a man like you kill except for love of something?"

Eugene picked up a pear, scraped some dirt off with his finger. A little boy came from out of nowhere to play a quick game of peek-a-boo.

"Love of what?" Eugene asked.

"I don't know," Nicole said.

"Well. You better find out."

"Yes," she said. "I will."

Eugene stood up. Took two steps away.

"Paris has been good for you," he told her.

"It hasn't really been anything for me yet."

"No," he said. "You look good. A little older. Your clothes fit better. Your sister's rubbing off on you."

"No," Nicole smiled.

"Who do you see here?"

She shrugged, bit off a piece of cheese.

"No men?"

"I see you."

Eugene brushed a few crumbs off his jeans.

"What do you do mostly? Are there things that you do?"

"I wait for you."

He said nothing.

"Eugene?"

"Yah?"

"I have not seen your room."

"No."

"I will make dinner for you tonight. In your room. Okay?"

"Okay."

At eight o'clock Eugene answered the knock at his door. It was Nicole. She wore a dress, a simple black dress, to the knees. There was no belt or tie, but it clung to her at her waist, and when she stepped through the doorway, the beautiful lines of her body were clear and distinct. Nicole had on open-toed shoes with a thin double strap around her heel; they made her an inch taller and made her legs look perfect. He could see the outline of her thigh under the cloth, and his eyes went up the rest of her body. She smiled at him confidently, almost arrogantly, but nicely, and then it turned to an all-nice smile. She wore no jewelry, no makeup. Her hair was shorter than it had been in Sancerre and was straight, some of it brushed to go behind her ears. Her smile faded slowly as she watched him and she pulled in her lips, then puffed out her cheeks and then just looked at him, cocking her head.

"I thought you were making dinner," he said.

She didn't answer.

"No food?"

She shook her head and then looked down and he touched her for the very first time. It was on her temple; he put two fingers there and held them, softly. Then his whole hand was on her cheek and moving down slowly to her neck. His nails went down the side of her neck, then one finger slid across her throat. He handled her delicately, gingerly, and when he kissed her she was surprised at the sudden strength. His hand was on her back, on her spine, and he held her to him, moving his hand, kneading her back, wasting not a movement. She grabbed his lips with her teeth; he almost laughed at the desperate suction at his tongue, and then they stopped kissing.

"We are going to make love," she said, and it was not a question nor hardly a command, but an almost bewildering expression of reality.

"Yes," said Eugene. And he thought, "Yes. Yes." And he also thought, "Why not? I've tried everything else."

Nicole smiled again. Radiantly.

He guided her to the bed, almost as if they were dancing. She slipped off her shoes and then her dress. She didn't even see him undress, she just knew he was kissing her shoulder; light, lingering kisses on her shoulder and then at the top of her breasts. And kissing her lips again and her nipples. His hands were perfect, they moved always to the right spot, always the right amount of pressure; still when wanted, moving when needed. He was on top of her, she could feel his entire body, they touched everywhere. And her legs went around him, up and down his back, and she saw his face, which was ecstatic; she saw his eyes which were focused only on his absolute pleasure; and her hands were all over him. Smoothing over his ribs, pulling at his beard and at his hair, sinking into his back and his buttocks. Then he was back on top and he nodded or she just knew it was right and she went to take him and put him inside her but he was already there. There was the slightest bit of resistance, which he liked, which made him grunt, but then he was in and her eyes widened, her mouth fell open, her nails went into his back, grabbed his head. She made noises, gasps, her eyes were closed. His were open, staring at her perfect face, then looking down at their two naked bodies, slithering together urgently, importantly, pleasurably. She could feel he was going to come which was all right, which was fine. He did, for a long time while she kept moving, drawing every last bit of pleasure until his hand touched her back and she knew he didn't want her to move anymore. The weight of his body came down on her, which she loved. She held him firmly, yet not too tight. His face buried itself in her neck. He kissed her once, quickly, in her hair. He rolled off her, rolled onto another pillow, lay on his back.

They didn't say anything for a long time. He coughed twice; she didn't make a sound. She raised herself slightly and put her hand on his chest. He nodded.

"That was perfect," she said. "Wasn't it?"

He sank down a little lower in the bed.

"Yes," Eugene said. "Yes it was."

"What will it be like from now on?" she asked.

He said nothing.

"It will be perfect," Nicole said. "It will be perfect."

There was another long silence, their bodies were just barely touching, which felt exactly right.

"I will tell Hélène now. That you're here."

He raised his eyes.

"I will quit school, I think."

He reached for his thin cigar. Lit it.

"I'll move out of their apartment. Now I'll have a real place. Where you can come."

He exhaled a mouthful of smoke.

"You will like some of my friends."

He inhaled more smoke.

"What shall we do tomorrow?" Nicole asked.

They made love twice more that night. Each time Eugene lasted a long time, each time he gave her as much pleasure as he could. Early in the morning, exhausted, exhilarated, drained, alive, Nicole kissed Eugene and said she would go home. She made plans for them to meet that night. At a café, near her house. She kissed him one more time, on the cheek, and he smiled very softly at her. He kissed her on both cheeks and she went home.

That night, Nicole sat outside at the café, waiting for Eugene. She looked beautiful, shining. She sat looking out onto the sidewalk and she was a statue with wonderful eyes. Gray eyes which turned in several directions, then down at her watch. Then back out to the street. And then, two hours later, when, over the telephone, the man at the hotel told her Eugene had checked out, that he had left Paris, Nicole's gray eyes were hurt and confused. And soft. And still. And way down, deep inside, underneath the layers of youth, dead.

Part Three

18.

A New York winter can go two ways.

Cold, it'll be cold—that's a certainty—but the temperature can be thrilling. The foot-stomping and the hand-clapping while walking down the street result from shivers of excitement and anticipation. The bad Salvation Army bands, the bells that are always ringing somewhere behind a conversation, the fanatical playground basketball players dribbling through midnight slush, the mittens and the mufflers and the frozen hard ground and lakes in Central Park— these can all add up to a season of twenty-degree cheer, an off-white security blanket.

Fireplaces with Perma-blaze logs, spindly dogs with their silly little woolen sweaters, stopping in a bar for an impromptu early evening Irish coffee. Fifth Avenue and the miraculous windows and Macy's with memories of Edmund Gwenn smoothing out the world's rough edges. Normally chalk-white faces turn red and look healthy; small, otherwise unappealing apartments take on a sense of warmth and protection; the air clears and the night-life lights up in alluring red and green and yellow flashes through dark gray skies. There are times when even the snow sticks and stays white and makes perfect snowball-warfare material.

Sometimes, when alone, fighting the wind, eyes half-closed, a slim edge of neck painfully exposed; lost in thought, in dreams, lost in the second-to-second battle for survival, it can be so fantastic the satisfaction is intoxicating. New York in winter, without stretching the imagination too far out of shape, can be considered a chilling heaven, a numbing montage of sensations. It can drive you to heights that no place else, at any other time, can possibly push you near.

Or it can be a killer.

The worst. The pits. The lowest. It can oppress like no other city would ever dare; freeze not only exposed ears and cheeks but *souls* that risk coming up to participate in life.

Baaaaaaadddddd. It can be real bad.

Ugly and penetrating. Cruel. A killer.

This one was not a great winter for Eugene.

For one thing, the Knicks sucked. Worse than that, they were just average, able to beat the weak teams most of the time, incapable of beating the Celtics or the Warriors or anybody with a really good center. The papers were even getting on Clyde, and they *never* dared go after The Man before.

All of which might have been tolerable, but the Giants had been unwatchable—tickets were *given* away during the season—and the Jets were even worse. Joe Willie was without a front line and a brash immortal was shown up on Monday Night Football to be an aging cripple.

The Rangers forget about; who *really,* deep down in their heart of hearts, cares about the Islanders; the Nets were ABA, which didn't count. New York was shut out. No winners.

There was a garbage strike. The smell was awful.

Old politicians were resurfacing, making their egomaniacal lunges for power. New politicians were smiling and promising their way to success. The odor was even worse than that of the garbage.

There were no good films out. Theater was dull. Jazz had quieted down.

Things were expensive and the city was going broke. No cops on the street. Good stores now had buzzing systems before it was even possible to browse. The snow was always deep and slushy, phones never worked, heat refused to come out of the pipes into apartments, no one trusted anyone else, no one really gave a shit about anything. Turn in any direction and there were crowds and crowds of people, directionless, blind, unknowing, a sense of overpowering desperation and terror hanging over them all.

There were no heroes left and none in sight, and there was nothing to look forward to and nothing to look back on. Which hit Eugene a lot harder than a minus-eighteen wind-chill factor.

Three times Eugene had been walking down the street, hit a patch of unsalted ice, and taken a full-fledged header.

It was not a good winter for Eugene Toddman, twenty-eight years old.

Eugene flew from Paris and had landed at Kennedy airport with two suitcases. Everything else he'd owned had been shipped back. After clearing customs he got a porter to take his bags to a taxi.

"Excuse me," Eugene said to the porter, "do you know what time it is?"

The porter was not particularly friendly.

"How the fuck should I know?" he asked. "You buy me a goddamn watch, I'll know the time!"

Eugene thanked him and hopped into a cab. Thanks to the traffic it took almost two hours to get into the city.

He went to a hotel, a good hotel, in the East Fifties. He tipped the bellboy well and collapsed on the bed. He lay there for forty-five minutes without falling asleep.

He called his lawyer.

"Gene," his lawyer said. "I was just talking with Miriam about you. We were just wondering what happened to you. Did you have a good trip?"

"Great," said Eugene and then listened as his lawyer explained all about taxes and shelters and investments and most importantly, that Eugene didn't really have as much money as he seemed to be spending.

"You spend a fortune, kid. You got nuthin' comin' in. It's murder. You don't wanna have to touch your capital, do ya?"

Eugene said he didn't.

"Okay, boychick. We'll talk. We'll have lunch. We'll hit the Friar's for a schvitz, okay?"

Eugene said okay and hung up.

He was back in New York.

He stayed.

He took an apartment, furnished it sparsely. And slowly, life came creeping back into him. New York refused to allow him to die without a struggle. He went to parties, saw a play here and there. Bought a new winter coat, leather and fur.

People were actually glad to see him. He was invited to play some indoor tennis and played squash for the first time. One woman taught him how to play backgammon. He liked the game but refused to learn anything about it, insisted on playing strictly by luck. Sometimes he won. Sometimes he lost.

He found himself getting his hair carefully styled, visiting his old manicurist. He listened to music constantly, Mozart mostly, and he never read or thought about what he *had* read and he never talked much. Didn't even do much listening. He watched a lot. But he hardly ever talked anymore. He came in contact with people and was able to slide right off them, leaving no impression, receiving no shock waves from the collision.

Eugene moved through his formless existence as gracefully as was humanly possible. He was an expert.

And so he passed through his first winter, Knicks and Namath and all, and then came spring.

It was a welcome relief, the initial warmth and the green. It was nice to hear baseball games on the radio. Seaver always gave the Mets a glimmer of early season hope. And the Yanks now had the Catfish and a definite winning team. Eugene played softball in the park. Sometimes he pitched, sometimes he played third base. He couldn't believe the price of baseball gloves.

Summer was hot and humid and strange because Eugene
didn't like the Southern accents he was hearing all over the
place—on TV, on the radio, on the streets—and he was
suspicious of the red, white, and blue wave of hope and
good feeling that was becoming infectious. He didn't think
Amy Carter was cute.

Autumn was really no different from summer, only cool-
er. Eugene stocked up on turtlenecks and jeans and Frye
boots and even found out that his down jacket was "in." He
didn't vote in the election. He was more concerned that Ali
was losing it, was close to being beaten. Eugene hoped he
would retire before tarnishing memories of the Thrilla in
Manila, the Rope-A-Dope, the laughs, the beauty.

Winter appeared again and this one was a bitch. It was so
fucking cold that it was usually crazy to go outside. Carter
was the new President, but his fireside chats were boring,
his advisors were old hacks, his theories were uninspiring,
and the jokes about him weren't very funny. The Knicks
were worse than ever, even with their ridiculously high
payroll. They lost twenty-point leads and had no defense,
and even Eugene had to admit that there were probably at
least ten guards in the league who could go right around
Frazier without too much trouble.

The Nets joined the NBA and lost Doctor J. The Mets
refused to pick up any free agents. The Giants weren't any
better. The Yanks picked up Reggie, but it wasn't the same
knowing that each home run and each strikeout cost about
ten thousand dollars apiece.

Namath, after a humiliating season, passed through waiv-
ers.

New York closed up for this winter. There was an energy
crisis and several people in the Bronx froze to death. No one
in Eugene's crowd froze, but they didn't party much. They
didn't do much. They didn't see much.

Eugene wasn't seeing as many women as he had in the
past. One woman lived with him, although briefly. Stayed
with him was more like it. It lasted three weeks and he

thought that was pretty good. He didn't miss her when she moved out.

Winter dominated everything, even Christmas, which Eugene spent with a small crowd. The shops didn't have their usual vitality, and some of the Santa Clauses even turned out to be Hare Krishna people in disguise. So Eugene was glad to see January come and then the beginning of February.

And then another party.

It was a very hip party. Actors and actresses, writers, producers. Mostly people in their early thirties up to early forties who made a fortune putting down the established order of things only to create their own order, perhaps a stronger and more enveloping system than had ever been established. One without a core. And without leaders. Without direction. An undefined system that seemed to just greedily spring out from the history of the world, controlling lifestyles, political movement, emotions, thought, and action.

There was some breast-feeding going on at the party, and lots of coke was being snorted off of delicate silver spoons or through tightly rolled bills. Everybody snorted these days; it was almost as middle class as grass. And people were *drinking* again in this era of post-Watergate morality. Tequila sunrises had become the martinis of the seventies.

Mike Bennett was mentioned several times, and Stephen Sondheim. People who couldn't name more than two songs on *Blonde on Blonde* discussed Dylan's *comeback*. Rebels had become superstars and star-fucking was an acceptable pastime. Nineteen-fifties TV was the rage. Groucho was young again, Bilko roared still, Ralph Kramden and Ed Norton bungled their way through Raccoon Lodge meetings. The 1960s were sentimental memories, mocked in films, degraded in print. As the gap between generations grew narrower, nostalgia extended to eras that many were unaware had even passed into oblivion.

There was no real fashion standard anymore. Some men's hair was long, some short, a decent amount of the fags had their concentration-camp cuts. Leisure suits had replaced togas as the official uniforms of a decaying civilization.

The women at the party considered themselves an oppressed

minority. Most of them wore expensive jeans, a few wore long skirts. There were a lot of high boots marching around or dancing to disco music. People hustled and bumped and had their love hijacked. A lot of them went *God! I still can't believe it's another year* and joints were passed around while one group went into orgasmic moans when they heard there were soapers being distributed.

A couple of people were fucking in a bedroom. On top of all the coats.

Four people were fucking in the den.

There was not a pair of straight pants in the apartment. Sixty percent of the attendees were est graduates. They never thought of infringing on anyone else's space or experience, they still thought it was possible to do their "own thing." They used the soul handshake. Not many of the couples were married. A lot were living together. Most of them had pets or expensive furniture or maids or plants or *something*. The structure of relationships had altered with the years, but the basic concept had not yet eroded. Possession was still considered a necessity, people willingly surrendered themselves to *things* to justify their belief in one-to-one communication.

Most of them were unhappy. Or would be unhappy soon.

It was a sophisticated bunch. Oh yeah. Some college professors with thinning hair down their backs and scuffed brown shoes. A few SoHo artists in army fatigues. A few women with big tits who were chasing, with equal fervor, Ph.D.s and any man who would respect and support them. Europe had definitely been covered, and parts of the Far East, Israel, Mexico, and the Islands. They all talked about being free, most of them felt they *were* free, or would be after a little more analysis. Most were comfortable. Read bestsellers, occasionally venturing into something more substantial. Like *Passages*. Many of them had seen all eight parts of *Roots*.

Most of them thought anything was okay, most of them would *try* anything, within reason. Most of them didn't know the difference between style and money or right and wrong or good and bad.

Hell, they were just people. They did okay.

They survived.

And at nine-thirty sharp, Eugene walked in to mingle with the survivors. Recognized a few people, nodded at some. Went to the bar for some mulled wine. Checked out the scene.

He neither hated the party nor had a particularly good time. He picked up no danger signs, felt no threat, had no urge to uncheck and unleash his self upon either his friends or his environment. Or upon the world. He was there and he stayed, smiled every so often, stayed on the fringe of several conversations, heard a few jokes, even told a few stories. He ate hors d'oeuvres, didn't bother to drift away or remove himself. He, too, was finally surviving, he decided. And he had decided that that was the thing to do. Survive and make sure others *let* him survive.

His decision-making was interrupted as someone tapped him on the shoulder. A man. Tall, older, perhaps in his late forties, very dapper, smoothly handsome. Graying hair, long in back, curling down over the top of the ears. The man wore a cashmere turtleneck, crushed velvet jeans, black Gucci shoes. The man looked French. He *was* French, and Eugene realized that he'd seen him before, that he knew him. Eugene narrowed his eyes and tried to decide whether to be scared or relaxed or aloof. His mouth opened a little, but he said nothing. The man spoke.

"Eugene?"

Eugene didn't answer, he swallowed. His mind flashed through a list of names, stopped when he came to Luce, knew that they'd met and talked at the Wickeses' party. The man addressed him again.

"*Bonjour*, my friend."

"Hello."

"I suspected that was you."

Eugene still had not acknowledged recognition. The man tried again.

"We met briefly. Two years ago. At a party given by Henri and Elise Wickes."

Eugene's mouth opened a crack, then closed before any words came out. He wet his lips and Paul Luce picked up nothing from his eyes.

"Perhaps you don't recall."

Eugene chewed on the inside of his lower lip and rubbed his palm against a pant leg.

"Yah. I recall. I remember. How are you? *Ça va?*"

"I'm very well."

"That's great."

"You've been gone from France a long time, no?"

Eugene nodded. Behind Luce, across the room and to the left, he saw a beautiful woman.

"What have you been doing?"

"What?"

"What have you been doing since you left Sancerre?"

The woman moved closer and Eugene could see she was magnificent. Elegant and stylish. Sexy, but youthful and innocent.

"Um . . . nothing, really."

"You've done *nothing?*"

She had dark hair that curved over her forehead and fell gracefully down her neck, just touching her shoulders. Her arms were long and slender. As she walked, they moved like dancer's arms, telling some unknown story each time they extended or bent or even just jiggled. She was a work of art with jeans tucked into high boots, a face colored by exactly the right amount of makeup, a hat that flopped in the proper places.

"Well, not *nothing.*"

"People wonder about you sometimes, in Sancerre."

"I traveled."

"It must be nice to travel for two years."

The woman was now coming toward him. He examined her face, to see if it measured up to his first impression of perfection. He knew it would and it did. Soft, smooth cheeks, beautiful features.

"Yeah. It is."

"My wife insisted we come to New York. She says she feels drawn, that New York will reveal some great secret. She has never been."

Her lips were French-actress lips. Her eyes looked out over the party, wide and curious, searching, and, he noticed, somehow sad. She walked at him and he understood her eyes. He understood the woman, for he had understood the girl.

"Monsieur Luce, did she come with you from France?"
Paul Luce turned to follow Eugene's gaze.

"Well, yes. Of course."

"Nicole Wickes."

"No longer."

Eugene twisted his head, cocking it to look at the Frenchman. He sensed what was coming. And it came proudly.

"She's Nicole Luce now. My wife."

And she was upon them.

"Nicole, look who it is. You remember Eugene Toddman, of course."

"Yes, of course. *Bien sûr.*" She looked him up and down. "I thought I recognized you." A congenial smile flickered. It faded.

Eugene wanted to take her hand. Just to hold it or something. He thought her hand might give some sudden comfort. Their eyes met and he smiled delicately, taking a step forward, but she broke the silence, turning to her husband.

"Paul, I have a terrible headache. Do you mind if we go back to the hotel?" She leaned over and whispered something in her husband's ear. He nodded and rolled his eyes exaggeratedly at Eugene.

"My wife," he muttered tolerantly. "She insists we come to New York for these mysterious reasons of her own, and she's ill every day we stay."

He spoke to Nicole again.

"Wait here and I will get your coat."

Paul Luce disappeared into the crowd. Mrs. Luce and Eugene Toddman stared at each other.

"Where are you staying?" he asked.

"Hotel," she said. And when he wanted to know *which* hotel, she daintily chewed off a fingernail.

"Let me give you my phone number and address," he said.

"No need," she replied. She glanced down and then looked directly at him. "I have them already."

She expected his eyes to gloat, to sparkle triumphantly. Instead they watered, only a bit, almost unnoticeably. But she noticed.

"The past repeats itself," she said.

"Does it?"

"Maybe not." She tilted her hat.

"I knew you were coming tonight."

"Did you?"

"Yes."

"I'd like to see you, Nicki."

"No one calls me that anymore. It's Nicole." She smiled coldly at him, tugged at her hat. Paul returned.

"Here you are, my dear." He kissed her lightly on the neck. Nicole slipped into her coat.

"Eugene," said Monsieur Luce, "I hope we get to see each other while we're here. Perhaps dinner."

Eugene smiled and nodded, shook hands with them both. Before they were out the door, Eugene heard Paul Luce say, "He looks well, don't you think?"

And he heard Nicole Luce say, "No."

Eugene left the party a few minutes later.

Three days passed and Eugene received no word from Nicole.

He paced up and down and bit his nails, peeled away at his cuticles, sat around nervously twisting his foot. He would get up and check to see what was in the refrigerator, would finger a Pepsi, put it back, close the door without taking anything, then check again fifteen minutes later. He read *Time* magazine from cover to cover. Twice. Tapped his fingers, chewed his lip. He took a few showers. Made a lot of phone calls. The first day he went out for meals, the second and third day he didn't leave the apartment. Just waited.

Four days after he had met Nicole at the party, Eugene was awakened by the sound of his doorbell. One eye opened at the harshness of the buzzing, his mouth was dry as he squinted at the ten-A.M. sun. The sound jarred him again and Eugene fully gained his sense of awareness, coming out of that half-dreaming, half-seeing first-thing-in-the-morning fog. He wondered who would be at his door and then he realized who it must be so he got moving. He hopped out of bed, pulling on a pair of perfectly faded jeans. He hesitated for a moment over a shirt, and as he yelled for his visitor to wait a minute, he chose a white turtleneck which he pulled on and smoothed over. Hopping into the bathroom, he grabbed his comb and stroked it through his tangled hair. Satisfied, Eugene looked into the mirror and grinned a hollow grin at himself.

He took a deep breath, walked to the door, opened it, and waited for Nicole to step in.

No one entered, so Eugene peered around the door, and there was a gangly kid busy picking his nose. They stared at each other.

"You Toddman?" he asked.

Eugene nodded.

"Thisiz fa you."

"Yeah."

They swapped two quarters for one small hotel envelope, and Eugene closed the door on the messenger's splotchy face. He ripped at the paper and found a small leafy piece of stationery with Nicole's married name printed in script at the top. There was a short note in her handwriting. "Come tomorrow at eight-thirty." That was all. No signature.

Eugene stared at the envelope, reread the line, carefully placed the message on a coffee table. He stifled a yawn, ran his fingers through the back of his hair, clutching and pulling it tight. He coughed, then belched, not much of a belch, then wondered how he could possibly make it through till eight-thirty the next night.

He made it, of course.

Thanks to a haircut, the revised version of the "Match Game," an unexpected ticket to see the Rangers, and Mozart.

Two hours before the appointed rendezvous, Eugene took a shower and dried his hair carefully, blowing it out to look perfect. He picked out an all-black outfit. Black turtleneck and pants, flared over black boots with one-inch heels. Eugene had been clean-shaven for a while during the warm weather. Now his beard was back, trimmed close and not quite full on his face. His eyes were piercingly blue and he knew it as he pulled on a heavy gray serape, wrapping it once over his right shoulder. Eugene stuck a chewed-off Brazilian stogey into his mouth, lit it, dangled it from his lip, and headed uptown.

At eight-fifteen he knocked on her hotel-room door. It opened a crack and Nicole was there blinking at him.

"Hello," he said.

"You're early," she countered.

He stood still and the door opened a little wider.

"Oh, come in, I suppose," she said. "I'll be dressed in a few minutes."

He stepped into a tastefully furnished suite as Nicole, clothed only in a towel, bounced into one of two dressing rooms. Eugene could see the moisture from her bare feet cling to the floor. He stood outside her dressing-room door, shuffling from one foot to the other, his cigar no longer burning.

"How have you been, Eugene?" she called in.

Eugene didn't answer. He studied the rust-colored carpet. He coughed. He bit his lip. He nudged the door with his boot and stepped into the room with her.

Nicole was looking into the mirror, applying a small dab of eye-shadow. She was still wearing the towel but it had slipped enough to fully reveal one absolutely flawless breast. Her legs were long and smooth, her toenails were painted red.

Eugene said nothing. Stared at her. He swallowed and his muscles tensed, he could feel his pulse. He thought, for one, brief, terrified moment, that he might start crying again. Nicole made no move to cover herself up, made no acknowledgment of Eugene's presence.

"Tell me what's happened," he said. "Since . . ."

Their eyes met and held. He didn't finish his sentence.

She flicked her glance over him, as if finally surprised that he was there, and she looked at him uncomprehendingly. Returning to the mirror, she finished with her eyes, then turned back to the man she had once thrown herself at, had once been willing to sacrifice her very being for, had once wanted to protect and shelter and love and worship. The man she once wanted to save her. She coolly let the towel drop, reached over and lifted up a simple black dress. The tip of her tongue ran over her lips, her stomach moved outward, caved in. She held the dress out and stepped into it, slowly draping her arm over her shoulder and down her back to run the zipper up to the nape of her neck. Eugene stood and watched, his right hand rubbing up and down his stomach.

"You've gotten fat," she said.

"A little bit. Not too bad."

He cleared his throat and noticed a scuff mark on one of his boots. He started to speak again but there was a knock at the door.

"*Oui?*"

"My pet," said Monsieur Luce, "the guests are arriving."

"I am talking with Eugene, Paul. He's watching me put on my makeup. We'll be out *tout de suite.*"

"I thought . . ." Eugene let his words trail off. He picked up a tiny bottle of Nicole's perfume.

"What?" she asked.

"I th . . . thought . . ." His words were thick, they stuck in his throat, and he stammered. He put down the perfume. "I didn't know your husband would be here. I didn't realize there were guests."

"There usually are at a party."

It was winter and yet she wore a summery dress. Designer quality. With arms and shoulders bared. He stared at her dangling silver earrings and tried to voice his thoughts once more.

"I . . ."

"Come," she said. And guided him into the main room.

It was a dressy affair, the men all wore suits, a couple even strode in with tuxedos. Eugene, in his casual attire, made subdued apologies which everyone accepted good-naturedly.

He was the only one there without a partner and, as they sat down to dinner, there was slight confusion over where to place him. The heat was turned on too high, he started to squirm in his sweater. His French was rusty and he couldn't quite keep up with most of the conversations. He stared at Nicole throughout the evening, thought of nothing but *her.* Her change, her growth, her onetime childish love for him. He thought of how he had left her.

He thought of how he wanted her now.

The party broke up but Eugene lingered till he couldn't

stay any longer. All evening he had tried to catch Nicole's attention, tried to speak to her, but she was constantly surrounded and he never managed. When it came time to leave, he shook Paul's hand and saw Nicole disappear into another room. Out in the hallway, alone, he tried to light up a cigar, but his hand shook and he couldn't. He threw away the matches.

The next morning he called her. The hotel switchboard answered so Eugene left his name and number, saying he would be home all day. She didn't call back.

The day after, he called earlier in the morning, but was forced to repeat the entire irritating process.

The following day he called every hour on the hour. Still she refused to contact him, still she was silent. He spent his days thinking about her, and at night he dreamt of her.

He was obsessed. Possessed. He was going nuts. Dreaming of the past, envisioning the future. He closed his eyes and he saw her pouting or smiling or beckoning him onward. He opened his eyes and he conjured her up, a vision of magic and tenderness and compassion. He heard her voice, smelled her, sensed the softness of her pale skin. He ran his fingers through her hair.

He wrote her a letter. There was no salutation.

This will be a funny letter to receive, for you. It is a funny letter to write, for me. Does that strike a chord in your memory? Do you cry at memories now, Nicki, or must you laugh at them?

I haven't seen you for a long time. ''Seeing'' means talking to, feeling for, understanding. Yet—and this realization came to me in a flash the other night when I realized that *you* were the alluring woman under the wide-brimmed hat—you have been a part of me for the past two years. I have carried your innocence and your love and your desire with me wherever I've been. The past has clung to me, much to my horror. Action upon action, deed upon deed, thought upon thought—they have cumulatively built the despairing robot I have become. I thought I could throw off the past in one grand gesture (murder being the grandest gesture of all—what could be a more impressive rejection of history than separating a piece of someone's forehead from the rest of his body, causing his brain to screech to a halt, forcing his impulses to scatter and die?). That's what I thought. But no way. No fuckin' way. Just as one action cannot mold, one action cannot disavow or erase. Or even simplify. All one action can do is begin another action. And then another. And then, somehow, incomprehensibly, a life.

I think often of our conversation in the woods. I'm sure I've forgotten most of what was actually said, but what the hell. We probably were understanding only ourselves anyway. And things come out much nicer when time's reinterpretations are added. I do know you trembled. And that I was afraid. And that you were too perfect for me to destroy.

I don't think often of Paris. Of that last day. I shouldn't have let you get away. The freedom I had disgusted me, but I couldn't do without it. It's strange what we'll sacrifice for freedom, or at least what we consider freedom. Happiness, trust, comfort. And it's a pity that all such sacrifices eventually lead nowhere, that they must always be looked upon as noble failures. It's an odd thing, to be a noble failure. And ultimately the most unsatisfying thing I could have become.

I've settled a lot since we last touched. I found out where Lenny's parents lived, and I sent them money. Not for long, though. Guilt never did become me. And it seemed such an empty gesture. So full of regret. I've not become a regretful person. Not yet, anyway. But I know what *has* happened to me. I've become a somewhat *sorrowful* person. I have joined the human race at last.

There are so many reasons why I left you. I was unworthy of what you had to offer. I'm probably still unworthy . . . but now I must have it. And need it. I must have and I need *you*. There. It's said. Ahh.

Time does many things to love . . . it distorts, deepens, saddens . . . but one thing it cannot do is destroy. Love is like a mystic energy. Its form changes but its core must always remain the same. You are a woman now. Solemn and understanding of so many things. Giving. Beautiful. You have seen the world now and it has put its stamp on you. But what you were has not died, merely been molded and shaped with age. No, you can't have changed. Still you must feel what you felt, desire what you desired, have what you wanted.

I have not wanted anything for such a long time. Why is it that life is only difficult if one insists on pursuing what is wanted? And why does it seem impossible that what we need and what we want can ever correspond to what we have?

Please.

Eugene

Eugene wrote out his message in ten minutes. When he was finished, he didn't reread his words. He rubbed his eyes and scratched his head, put the plea in an envelope and licked it shut.

He carried the letter over to Nicole's hotel, left it with an aging clerk at the front desk. Eugene looked terrible—and the clerk eyed him suspiciously. Eugene tried to straighten himself up under the scrutinizing glance but succeeded only in bumping into an elevator operator. Sweating, just a little, Eugene passed through the revolving doors back into the cold. He walked back to his apartment, staring at his reflection in store windows that he passed, clicked Mozart onto his turntable, fixed his gaze on a blank wall, and waited for the response he knew would come.

It didn't come.

No word from Nicole. Not a note. Not a phone call. Not even an angry quit-bothering-me-and-leave-me-alone quickie. Nothing. He was not worth her bothering with. He was beneath her contempt. Worse, he thought, he was forgotten. Forgotten.

Then he realized she must be out of town. The message couldn't have been delivered to her yet. He splashed some cold water on his face in relief, three days after he had borne her the note, and called the hotel to verify his realization. Mrs. Luce, they said, had *not* left town. Yes, the message had been delivered. No, she was not ill, in fact she was out shopping.

Eugene hung up the phone and fell back into a bulky chair. His hair was greasy and unwashed as he ran his fingers through it. He chewed on his lip, already chapped and blistered. His eyes were wide, looking at nothing, strangely crooked. His foot tapped, he bit his nails, he looked through his phone book and couldn't find anyone he wanted to call.

He felt as if he was coming down with the flu. There was

no strength, very little holding him up. He was hot and tired and beat. And his eyes just stared straight ahead, widening little by little, taking in more, seeing less.

He began calling Nicole regularly. Hourly. Sometimes the operator would say that Mrs. Luce was not in. Sometimes Paul Luce himself would come on the phone, apologetically and softly explaining to Eugene that he felt no animosity toward him, that his wife was feeling ill these days, that he must confess he had no idea what was going on, but please, *s'il vous plaît*, stop calling.

Eugene kept calling. Monsieur Luce told him that they were returning to France.

Eugene started to cry.

It was different than before, but he still couldn't help it. Not gasps of terror, not painful screams that tore from out of his insides. Just long slow draining tears that did nothing but empty him out further.

A clarinet concerto spun round on the stereo. Flowed softly throughout the apartment, slipped in and out of each room. The television was on with no sound. Window curtains hung haphazardly, some partway open, some closed and crumpled. Dishes were in the sink. Cups sat on tables or in ashtrays. Paintings hung crookedly, the refrigerator buzzed incessantly. Eugene's emptiness suffocated his home.

He sat for days.

Didn't even go out for meals. Hardly ate. Once or twice he went out for a paper but the wind whipped at his face and lashed at him and drove him, reeling, back inside. Leaning against the outer door to his apartment building, Eugene put his hand to his forehead and listened to his own quickened breathing. He heard himself moan. Suddenly he sprung around, as if to receive an army of muggers leaping up at him from the stoop. The street was empty, but violent images burst through into Eugene's sensibility. He felt invisible fists driving into his stomach, doubling him over, nonexistent knives slicing into his chest, his blood staining through his shirt. He fought back and did some damage, but as he felt himself succumbing, he quickly went through the front door and headed up to his apartment.

Stepping through his living room, he sank back in a leather easy chair. Head down, eyes half-closed, hands shaking, expression absolutely blank. He sat for an hour or two. Dragged himself up eventually and went off to bed, pulling three blankets round his shoulders.

The day came for Nicole's departure. Eugene had gotten their check-out date from the hotel clerk. As he woke up that morning, Eugene was alone, and worse, was lonely. He drank a few cups of coffee. He even called his old pal, Casey. Casey was living with a girl now, they'd been together for a year. When Eugene called, Casey was in the midst of an argument with his better half. The two old friends had a strained conversation; they still cared for each other but more than anything it was as a tie to simpler times, as a memory of an irreplaceable space in a different life. Casey didn't sense the urgency in Eugene's voice, he said he'd have to call back, when they could talk longer. Eugene hung up the phone, coughed, lit up a cigar. He called Nicole; there was no answer in her room. He left no message, went into the kitchen, and heated up a piece of Sara Lee's banana cake. A cold was definitely upon him, he popped some Vitamin C. He waited for something to happen. As he'd always waited.

The doorbell rang. Just once. Eugene, barefoot, in a T-shirt and jeans, blew his nose, opened the door. Nicole walked in.

The first thing Eugene noticed was that she was wearing sunglasses, he couldn't see her eyes. Then he noticed she looked wonderful. Perfectly put together. Her outfit was dressy, a three-quarter-length skirt and a white puffy blouse. Brown boots. Expensive. Her hair was loose and hung naturally. She said nothing. Eugene blinked and blew his nose again.

"You are sick." She spoke softly and, he was sure, tenderly.

"Just a cold."

"You never used to get sick."

She was so serious he couldn't help but smile.

He said, "In all the years we spent together, you mean?"

She walked around his living room, examining objects, touching furniture, looking as if she were trying to memorize the proper place for each and every item. She strode into his bedroom, he waited for her to come out. She briskly moved through the rest of the apartment. Stopped back in front of Eugene.

"You don't cook?"

"Not much. Eggs sometimes. Or coffee or something."

"You don't clean much either."

"Uh uh. Not much."

"What *do* you do?"

"What?"

"What do you do with your time?"

"What did I *ever* do?"

"I don't know. *Je ne sais pas.*"

Their eyes met. She was positive that Eugene's mocked her ever so faintly, daring her to reach into him and drag out that force that moved him forward, counterclockwise to life's mainstream and to her existence.

"You used to know everything about me."

She took her glasses off. Her eyes were gray and hollow. Strong yet uncertain. Withdrawn, forlorn. Holding back. Afraid. Determined. So sad.

"No," she said. "I never."

Eugene's cold seemed to be getting worse. He sniffed mucus in through his throat and rubbed two fingers across his nose. They came away wet and a little sticky. He wiped his hand across his thigh.

"Why did you want to see me?" Nicole asked. She spoke in short syllables that burst into terse sentences. When Eugene didn't answer, she took off her coat and folded it across the back of a chair.

"Why did you want to see me?" she said again.

"Would you like come coffee?" Eugene asked. "I make it with cinnamon."

Nicole just stared at him, arms crossed over her chest. He disappeared into the kitchen, came out a minute later with a mug of black coffee, which he sipped. He looked up at her, pushed his hair back off his forehead, away from his eyes.

"I wanted to see you," was the best he came up with.

"I know. I'm here. *Pourquoi?*"

Eugene shrugged.

"Still you live by riddles."

Eugene felt flush, feverish, and his eyes were a bloodshot

mess. They looked like tiny road maps. He spread his arms in front of Nicole.

"I don't think I live by *anything* anymore."

"What do you want?"

Eugene coughed, ran his hand up and down his Adam's apple.

"You," he decided.

She turned. Mechanically. Faced him directly. A confrontation.

"That first day I saw you," Nicole intoned, "you were something to see. You had this look on your face, like you were absolutely *disgusted* being alive if you had to live in this *shit*."

"Yeah, well," Eugene coughed. "My love of mankind has been pretty well documented."

"Yes. I thought you were fabulous. It was all in your eyes. Your . . . *merde, comment est-ce qu'on dit* . . . *aberrant* . . . your revulsion and your tolerance and your ability to despise and to love at the same time."

He smiled now, nodding, remembering.

"It *is* possible to love without liking," he said, and he had to leave the room to get another handkerchief. He returned with a photograph that he shielded in the palm of his hand.

"From that moment until now, Eugene, I lived only to see, in your eyes, *love* and nothing else. I wanted to be the one to make you pure. I thought I had. In Paris. But no. I knew it, too, I knew it. I hoped, but deep down I knew I had failed."

He had nothing to say. His throat hurt; he rubbed the edge of his palm around puffed glands.

"You suffered so much. Not knowing what to share, what to offer. Not knowing what to do with your knowledge. Not knowing how to survive with truth beckoning at you as if you alone could perceive it. I wanted to be the one to share your suffering," she said.

And he smiled again, a rare smile, this time a gentle one, and he cast his eyes downward. "And with your sharing, do away with it?"

"Yes."

"Ahhhh."

"Yes. Ahhh."

"I don't know. It's funny, Nicole, maybe, how fragile beliefs are."

"And how ultimately ridiculous."

Eugene wanted to hold her, place his arms around her and rub his hand over her back to reassure her that things were all right. But while her words were revealing, impassioned, her tone was distant, unemotional. This was the woman of twenty, not the girl of seventeen, and she seemed not to want to be comforted.

"Leave your husband and come with me," he said.

"And where would we go?"

"I don't know."

"What would we do?"

He shrugged.

"Pick a place."

He thought. "Africa."

"I don't like it there."

They didn't speak for maybe two or three minutes. A long time. She stared at him. He scratched and shuffled and sniffed and coughed.

"Look what I have," he said finally, and held out his hand.

Nicole picked the photograph out of his palm, his sweat helped it slide easily to her.

"It's a picture of you," he went on. "It's when . . . right before I left . . . the day I left Sancerre. I saw you in the street. You were buying some food. I went into a store and bought a camera and followed you and took your picture."

Nicole looked uninterested. She flipped the photograph onto his couch, kept her eye on it as it settled on top of a pillow, face down.

"I left right after that. I was leaving . . . that's why I didn't say anything to you. Just followed you. Look how young you were. Look at that. Like Paris. You were so beautiful that night. The most beautiful . . . you were . . ."

Eugene stopped. Nicole started to fidget with her coat.

"At one time you wanted to go off with me *wherever* I went."

"That was one time."

"And you've changed?"

"The time has changed."

He couldn't help himself now; his eyes welled up with tears. He kept blinking them away and started to cough to cover up the fact that his voice was breaking. Nicole picked up her coat and pulled it around her. She put her sunglasses back on and surveyed the room once more; her hidden eyes went over every inch of Eugene's body. She shook her head, a tiny swaying movement, a flinch, and she took a few steps toward the door.

Eugene raised his voice and told her that he'd do anything. Said, well maybe not anything but he'd change. And go where she wanted to go, do what she wanted to do. He could be restored, he said, like a work of art. Touched up, rebuilt. He said they could go off together. He said that he loved her.

Nicole turned back. Like stone. When she spoke, her words came from a fury, a sore, within.

"You're weak," she said. "And you've offered me an insulting passion. You're not the same. Or maybe you are and I only just now see it. You have *nothing* to give, nothing to share. I'm married and maybe I'll have a child soon and I'm safe forever."

She wanted to leave but his eyes searched her, asked her questions and she stayed to answer his eyes.

"You could never offer me safety," she said. "You could never offer me anything except a moment of pleasure. And what is that? Nothing."

A gurgling sound escaped from Eugene's throat.

"I've found pleasure very disappointing," she said.

"And what about," said Eugene very carefully, "the *possibility* of pleasure?"

"Gone," Nicole said. "And I don't miss it."

The only sound in the room now was Eugene's heavy breathing.

"It is a great sorrow to me, Gene, to find that you're a fool like everyone else. You made me think that things were different than they really are, you made me think that you had a way of making real life out of lies. I came to New York to see you again. I searched for you. I had to find out what you'd become, what you'd found out, where your passion would lead you."

All strength floated away from Eugene's body. All support, all structure sagged, dissolved, disassociated itself from Eugene's being.

"I'm sorry your passion has led you nowhere," Nicole said. "It makes such a mockery of both our lives."

Her eyes were clear, her voice had been calm, her manner was relaxed and dispassionate. Nicole turned and walked to the door. She stepped out of the apartment, into the hallway, passed through the elevator, emerged onto the street, leaving Eugene to stand in his living room, riveted to his spot on the carpet and to the past and to the nothingness that enveloped and overwhelmed him.

Part Four

19.

In six hours Eugene Toddman was going to turn thirty.

In one hour Casey was going to be married. He had called to announce the good news.

"Congratulations," said Eugene.

"In two weeks," said Casey. "And guess what?"

"What?"

"The wedding's in New York. Laurie's from New York."

"Great."

"You'll be the best man."

"Okay."

"And guess what again?"

"What?"

"We're getting married the day before your birthday. Your *thirtieth*, buddy."

"I know."

"We're gonna be living in New York."

"You can work here?"

"Got a job already!"

"Designing?"

"No. Not really. Working for Laurie's father."

"Oh."

"He's a linen manufacturer."

"Sounds interesting."

"He supplies the linens for almost all the big hotels in New York."

"Ah."

"That's what I'll be in charge of."

Eugene didn't say anything.

"Gene?"

"Yeah?"

"You there?"

"Yeah." He needed one more short silence. "It sounds great, Case. I'm excited for you."

"Okay then. I'll see ya when I get to the city."

"Okay. See ya."

Now Casey was in town. And Eugene was about to turn thirty. In six hours.

He was walking to the wedding. He felt some energy building up inside him so he decided to tire it out of himself. He strolled down one of the great Village side streets; the trees were blooming purple and green, there was a slight breeze, so it was actually pleasant weather. He looked at his watch and saw he had plenty of time. He headed uptown. Lit a cigar.

He realized soon that he was near the apartment he first lived in with Mort. He never got around the neighborhood anymore, there was never any reason to. Quick bursts of youthful images attacked Eugene, skittered away. He imagined Mort as he was when they had lived in New York. Eugene felt a wave of sentimentality wash over him. An apparition of Mort as an older man then appeared before Eugene. He tried to shake it away, lose it admidst the traffic, but he couldn't. Eugene stopped for a second, took a deep breath. He looked up at the cloudless sky, then back down at the pavement's potholes. He felt a little funny and when he heard something rumble inside him he looked down dubiously at his stomach, not at all sure that was the source of the disturbance.

Mort killed himself, his son knew. At least did his very best to help his death along. He wanted too much. He wanted things to be like they were. Whenever. Eugene thought his mother did Mort a grave disservice by kicking off while they were happy. She made him believe that she was the reason for his happiness . . . and for his eventual unhappiness. Bullshit, Eugene decided. Relationships are extensions of the self, not definitions of the self. Eugene smiled, knowing he was right. Mort had never realized. And that's why he died a miserable fat drunk. He no longer knew what he was, so he no longer knew what he wanted. Mort had no longer known what he had. So he had nothing.

Eugene discovered he was already in the low Fifties. He walked over to Lexington and Fifty-third to the best egg-cream place in the city. He drank two chocolates, licked the delicious foam off his moustache, and realized that Mort had been a romantic, he had confused a moment with eternity. Eternity is only *composed* of moments. Some the way we like them, some not. Eugene decided that egg creams were definitely contributors to good moments. He paid his buck. Nicki was a romantic, he thought. And he was, too. Or had been.

He thought about Nicole and how it had begun. He crossed against the light and knew that he had never been much good with beginnings. Maybe that was why he'd always had such a hard time understanding endings. Walking along past a group of construction workers, it popped into Eugene's mind that endings had always meant death to him. So beginnings were always a form of rebirth. Probably his earliest misconception, he thought, and one of the most ill-formed of many. His mother died and he was born. A school chum died and he moved to California. His father died and he left California. Death had brought him money and mobility and it even whisked him out of a basement apartment and into some new landlady's fishcave. Eugene started whistling, but only got a couple of notes out before he admitted that he'd always left the dead behind him, hoping that they wouldn't follow. They did, of course; conceivably he had even brought them with him. But he started whistling again and felt good, and thought, Jesus, what a weird way to start feeling good. Death doesn't give meaning to life, he thought. Hell, *nothing* can do that. Death just *ends* it, is all. There are no rebirths, no real beginnings. There is, if you want to look at it negatively, postponement of the inevitable. Or,

positively . . . postponement of the inevitable. Hmmm. That
was the first thing, Eugene realized. But before he could get
on to number two, a doorman was asking him what apartment he wanted.

Eugene asked for Casey's fiancée's father's apartment
and was directed there. He took the elevator and found
himself walking into an unbelievable place. Large enough
to have a crowd of people. And a three-piece band. And a
dance floor. After hugs and kisses and various introduc-
tions, he struggled to return to his own mind. Nicole was
there, and the look on her face when he saw her last. It was
horrible. Sad and lost and unfeeling. It was an ugly mask,
and Eugene thought it was ridiculous that people would
bother to wear masks if they were ugly ones, at least if they
were uglier than what was really underneath. Preferable, by
far, to let the hideous truth shine through protective calm,
through smiling isolation. He was fast losing himself within
his own thoughts. He was barely conscious of his movements; the party, the world were becoming but shadows,
reflections of his mind. He felt suddenly strong. Stronger,
anyway. More solid than he had for quite a while. And he
reached back again, back inside him to see what was left,
but it was time for the ceremony. He was holding the ring
and listening to the judge pronounce the wedding vows.
Eugene saw a good-looking girl who was giving him the
eye. He smiled at her, he knew his eyes were working all of
a sudden, and for some reason he remembered the very first
time he'd ever masturbated.

He was playing "spy" all by himself and he was slinking
and crawling around from room to room on his way to
establishing justice throughout the entire free world. On one
of his slinks and crawls, he couldn't help noticing that there
was a strange, sticky, milky substance that had just come
leaking out of his pathetically throbbing male member. It
seems he'd been running it along the ground in his search
for pesky Russians and he'd inadvertently come for the first
time. It was quite a treat. He felt embarrassed, without
knowing why, but also delighted and, yes, no question,
manly and virile and grown-up—all without having any idea
at all of what he'd done. It sure felt good, though.

Eugene was forced to concentrate now on an introduction. To a woman, the one who'd been giving him the once-over, the maid of honor.

"She's an instructor at the Fred Astaire School of Dance," some friendly matchmaker was saying.

"Is that right?" said Eugene.

"Yes," the girl blushed.

"Would you like to dance then?" Eugene asked her.

"Watch out for him," someone laughed. "He's a real lady-killer."

They went through a foxtrot. Then another. Then a waltz. He knew she thought he was a good dancer. He led her smoothly around the room, and as soon as he felt her relax, he was back in his own mind. He fought it for an instant, tried to concentrate on what was real, what was momentarily real, but for weeks he'd known he'd been changing. Into what, he didn't know. He didn't know if it was good or bad. He didn't care. Something was happening again and he was excited. He'd be damned if he was going to stop it, so he drifted away expectantly, right back to where he'd left off.

It *had* felt good, that first time he'd stained himself with sperm, and, in one form or another, he'd probably been beating off ever since, he figured. He had figured that anything that could feel so good could somehow feel even better. The next step in his fatal logic: As Sartre said, if you can get laid, why slam the ham. So from playing camp under the covers with a flashlight, he moved onward. To search for something better. Always feeling good, always wanting something better. Soon forgetting he *had* something good, soon hating what he had. Soon living only for one day when the grin on his mug became a permanent fixture and his something better would be a dreamlike image who could discuss Proust, cook up some eggs Benedict as a midnight snack, isolate him from the world's banality, inject him with frenzied knowledge, and keep him hard enough to ride the Hershey Highway every waking minute—naturally doing all of this simultaneously.

Eugene knew it was his own egocentric view of the world that all men share the same fantasy, more or less. Underneath it all, beneath all the layers of civilization that prevent human beings from being human. The web that prevents the mind from leaping into a chasm of sensual pleasure, a guilt-free abyss of leisure and ease. And to be bold, include women in this perception of the Universe, for we're all bound by one common element—imagination. It's so difficult to cope with the modern world because so much of it is unreal, so much ethereal, so much a bit of an idea, a corner of a plan, a flash of an image—all made solid and believable. And thus real. Let passion peel away the age, and motherhood and art and religion and money would crumble like the myths they are. Ahhh, to be left with a bunch of naked people getting mouthfuls of hair under shady groves.

Casey and his bride were leaving. She tossed the bouquet of flowers, someone squealed with glee after grabbing it. Casey came over and hugged Eugene. He held him close, patted his back. Eugene shook the groom's hand.

"So what do you think of all this, Gene?"

"I'm happy for you."

"No. I mean . . . whaddya think of all this? The wedding. The people. My wife. Do you like my wife?"

"I hardly know her."

"An instant reaction. Do you like her?"

"Yes," said Eugene.

"You don't," said Casey.

"No," said Eugene.

"It doesn't matter."

"Look. What does?"

They grinned at each other and hugged again. The newlyweds disappeared and then Eugene was with Fred Astaire.

"We'll go out somewhere?" he asked her.

"I have to pick something up at work, first," she said. "It's not far."

So they went outside. She talked and he thought. He knew it was silly to believe in the Garden of Eden at this late date. This *is* the twentieth century and we all have to deal with tract homes and Billy Graham and David Bowie and the fact that a little box of Q-tips costs over a dollar. It made no sense anymore to discuss what was or what might have been or whether man is good, evil, or indifferent. Or whether life is just or fair or cruel, or God is avenging, omniscient, existing. God exists because there are too many people who *think* he exists. There are too many evil people in the world to *tell* whether man is evil or not. There have been too many wars, too many saints, too many countries, too much repression, too many books, too many *years* for *anything* to make any sense anymore. Those wacky existentialists say history isn't important. Probably. But what people have to understand is that it's the *whys* of history that no longer matter. Whatever the reason for the fall, we're fallen. And explanations aren't cures. The only way to work your way back to the mythical past is not to struggle against it but to *ignore* it.

And the next thing Eugene knew he was back in the midst of the mythical present, standing around in the middle of Fred Astaire's marble-columned waiting room. He watched an old man who wore one of the world's worst toupees glide through a waltz with a woman whose feet were covered with Band-Aids. The man was wrinkled, flabby, the skin around his neck sagged loosely. The woman was suffering, trying to look cheerful, smiling despite her corns and stepped-on toes. Eugene shifted his gaze. A fat girl, a teenager, smiled at him. She was missing a tooth. There were pimples up and down her arms. This other woman, around forty, was dressed all in black, trying her best to look like a slinky witch. She had all her teeth but several of them were pointed, sharp, ready to draw blood. She was busy running her hand up and down her thigh and calf. A blind man was attempting to learn the foxtrot. Eugene wondered what he looked like behind the sunglasses, whether his eyes were simply there but unseeing or whether they were burnt-out holes, empty shells, rotting flesh. Four or five fags in dinner jackets kept moving from couple to couple, watching their feet and posture, sometimes chipping in with a ''slow . . . slow . . . quickquick.'' One screamer asked Eugene if he was being helped. Eugene nodded.

''Da daaaa,'' said his date as she popped in front of him, her leg dramatically draped around one of the columns. ''I'm ready.''

Eugene lowered his eyes and smiled and they went for a drink that stretched into three, in a hotel lobby. With bright red, thick carpeting, long mirrors, enveloping leather furniture. Very plush. As the girl talked, Eugene watched the people crossing through the lobby. Two cripples came hobbling along. One alcoholic.

"I'm from the Bronx," the girl said.

"Yeah," said Eugene.

A cute young blonde was yelling with Herculean force at a rather weak-willed husband. A prostitute smiled at a businessman at the bar.

"I wonder why they call it *the* Bronx," Eugene's table companion said. "I mean, they don't call it *the* Manhattan, or *the* Queens."

Eugene watched the people go past out on the street. He counted four dope addicts. Eight fags, maybe three dykes. A helluva lot of ugly people went by, girls who'll have to settle for a small kitchen in Jersey if they want any shot at a life of connubial bliss. Minority members just fucking swarmed all over the place, begging or strutting or converting. It was amazing. Eugene just kept his gaze fixed upon one ordinary spot and all he saw were people, bent or stooped or twisted. Gnarled or confused or angry or rushing or dawdling. It was the biggest mess he could possibly imagine. The girl was talking and he didn't hear a word she said. He got this stupid grin on his face, he couldn't wipe it off, and he thought, so these are people, huh? And then he saw a few couples holding hands, a few checking film times. A few who were smiling or kissing someone. They didn't look that great to him either, but he just grinned and grinned and finished his drink and took the girl for Chinese food.

"It was a nice wedding, donja think?" she asked.

There was a piece of fried rice on her chin and Eugene was hoping it would fall down onto her tits. He concentrated, trying to make it fall.

"Oh sure."

Her tongue caught the rice and Eugene was disappointed, but a moment later she substituted a squared-off piece of pork and he resumed his prayers.

"She's a great kid."

"Great." Eugene nodded. "Great."

Whadda ya know, he thought. It's not so hard to stop looking at our lives as if life itself were a beautiful or an ugly thing. The best thing is to simply pick out the things we want as we meander within our own boundaries.

The girl was putting up a bit of an argument over whether to come down to his place and Eugene remembered when

Nicole disappeared from his apartment. His concept of eternity froze into one painful moment. Jesus, he had thought, I've lost something for the very first time. He wondered then how many losses it was possible to sustain and still remain whole. He had an answer now. A lot.

"I should go home, really. It's a long trip."

"Don't bother. You can stay at my place."

"Oh no. I should get back."

"Okay."

"Would it put you out?"

"No."

"I should get back."

"Okay."

"Well . . . do you have an extra room?"

He thought about Lenny. He tried to tear some grief out of himself but there was none there. He had been overcome with grief, for a while. But not for Lenny. Like all of us who get overcome with grief, it's for ourselves. Lenny got what he wanted. He died convinced that, in some strange way, honor had been upheld. And that's what he was all about. Honor and justice and structure and poetic endings in which everything deserving came to those who deserved. Eugene knew he had upset Lenny's sense of balance. He remembered that he had almost been able to feel Lenny thinking, in the split second before he collapsed, about the glory his death would bring him. The love and the dramatic mourning and the resulting order. Lenny lived by memory and Eugene was convinced he did nothing more than assure him his memory would be preserved. It wasn't, of course. It's a joke. But he's dead and will never know it. So how could Eugene force grief to come in? If he had to do it all over again, he wouldn't have bothered. But it's done. It's a completed action. There is no such thing as an incorrect action, for we do, ultimately, what we decide we want to do at a given moment. Eugene realized that if he'd known that at the time, Lenny would most likely still be turning out pages of bad poetry. For Eugene wouldn't have felt the need to strike out, wouldn't have felt threatened. He was powerful then, and he felt exposed and vulnerable. Aware of his powerlessness now, Eugene suddenly felt secure and impregnable. Actions are no longer a means to measure a man. He didn't think there *was* a way to measure a man. So why judge? And why struggle? Yes. Why not sidestep history by defining ourselves anew with every action? It could be exciting . . . the ultimate entertainment . . . dodging the past's tentacles to keep ourselves alive.

She was in his apartment, in his bedroom, she was unbuttoning her shirt.

"He wants a baby," she said.

"Who?"

"Casey. The groom."

"Oh. Yeah. I know."

She was taking off a stocking. She coiled the nylon around her ankle and then let it drop off her toes. Her legs were slim, sturdy. No wasted flesh.

"You think she wants a baby?"

"Sure."

"You think so?"

She was on her back, her legs up, perfectly together, at a forty-five-degree angle, and she pulled off her pants. He could see that she had a nice ass. He got horny.

"Sure," he said. "Everybody wants a baby, don't they?"

"Do you want a baby?"

"No."

His shirt was off now, and his shoes and socks. He was in better shape than he had been for some time. The rolls around his middle were at a minimum, his skin had a faint tan. His hair was long and looked good. His arms were strong. He stepped out of his pants and stood over the girl. Her heel touched his leg.

His thoughts had become time-fillers. Which he now thought was kind of nice. The thing was to be stimulated now during the moments when he wasn't having wine poured down his throat or hot showers taking the crimps out of his neck, or when he wasn't putting his tongue to its best possible use. Art is something to keep us from crying, or to keep us from committing a boredom-induced suicide. Ideas aren't reality, they're all-important diversions from reality, real in themselves, to be kept separate, at all costs, from our movement, our actions, our reactions. If the great artists had never existed, their thoughts still *would* have. There are no great

men; if we're lucky we just get men who do great things
occasionally.

"Do you respect women?" she asked.

Kneeling on the bed, he stopped. Froze. Stared at the
woman in his bed. At her naked body, her legs, hair, her
breasts, her flat stomach.

"What?" he said.

"Do you respect women?"

Nicole, he thought, I couldn't have kept you safe. You
were right. I wouldn't try, though. You turned down a momentary pleasure and here's what I've learned: If I could
have given you that, you should have snapped it up. They're
pretty hard to come by. And Eugene now looked at the girl
in the bed and laughed.

"No," he said. "I don't respect anybody."

The girl held out her arms.

"Love me to death," she said.

He was on top of her now, they were touching. Moving.
Joining. Understanding.

"It's a funny thing," Eugene said.

"What?"

He looked down at his watch and saw that he was now
thirty years old. He had lived his whole life moving from
moment to moment. And he was going to *keep* moving from
moment to moment. He was going to try, at least. No more
searching. Take what comes, grab out occasionally at something desired. And he knew that if he missed, he'd go for
something else.

"What's a funny thing?" the girl asked.

There is no secret. There are no answers. There's life and
there's death and you can choose one or the other. It was
pointless to pick the latter—it was bound to gobble *you* up
sooner or later. So do whatever the hell you want, he thought,
and forget about the consequences, but accept them when
they come or fight against them if you can. Accept the pain,
too, when it's real, and let your eyes dance and laugh at the
poor dead souls.

"What's a funny thing?" the girl asked again.

He wanted to see Nicole, just to tell her. Tell her what he
now knew. That love is the acceptance of mystery between

people, that we can only love till we understand. What is commonly called a relationship is actually the act of *trying* to understand. Some people are lucky enough never to succeed. Others are cursed with inescapable insight.

Eugene knew he couldn't touch other people without loving them. Nicki had been right. But he'd been so afraid of that love, couldn't love them without finally leaving them. He had always had the insane desire to eliminate an ending. All his life he'd been afraid to reach an ending.

That's what we're all afraid of, he wanted to tell Nicole. Endings. And ending. He wasn't anymore, he was sure. He wasn't looking forward to it. No way. But he wasn't trembling.

"Life," said Eugene Toddman.

And they lay still now, locked together, on his bed, and Eugene looked down at the girl, then at his own body.

"It's a funny thing."

ABOUT THE AUTHOR

PETER GETHERS *is presently living in New York City and working on his second novel.*

READ TOMORROW'S LITERATURE—TODAY

The best of today's writing bound for tomorrow's classics.

☐	14128	RAGTIME E. L. Doctorow	$2.95
☐	13433	THE SUMMER BEFORE THE DARK Doris Lessing	$2.95
☐	13441	ONE DAY IN THE LIFE OF IVAN DENISOVICH Alexander Solzhenitsyn	$2.50
☐	14061	THE END OF THE ROAD John Barth	$2.95
☐	2997	AUGUST 1914 Alexander Solzhenitsyn	$2.50
☐	13675	THE GOLDEN NOTEBOOK Doris Lessing	$3.95
☐	12581	MEMOIRS OF A SURVIVOR Doris Lessing	$2.50
☐	13888	THE CRYING OF LOT 49 Thomas Pynchon	$2.75
☐	13894	GRAVITY'S RAINBOW Thomas Pynchon	$3.95
☐	12545	BEING THERE Jerzy Kosinski	$2.25
☐	13370	V Thomas Pynchon	$2.95
☐	13619	THE PAINTED BIRD Jerzy Kosinski	$2.50

Buy them at your local bookstore or use this handy coupon for ordering:

Bantam Book Catalog

Here's your up-to-the-minute listing of over 1,400 titles by your favorite authors.

This illustrated, large format catalog gives a description of each title. For your convenience, it is divided into categories in fiction and non-fiction—gothics, science fiction, westerns, mysteries, cookbooks, mysticism and occult, biographies, history, family living, health, psychology, art.

So don't delay—take advantage of this special opportunity to increase your reading pleasure.

Just send us your name and address and 50¢ (to help defray postage and handling costs).